# While He Was Sleeping

ཡུལ་པ་

# CHRIS JOHNSON

# DEDICATION


Tony Evans
David Boulton
Daniel Logovik
Madame Alexandra David-Neel (original inspiration)
My high school English teachers
Dracula (such a pain in the neck)

# CHAPTER 1

The sudden knock at my bedroom door flicked me to the present. There, sweaty in his overalls from a day of roadworks, stood Dad. The look in his eyes told me. Dad had heard the news.

"Do you know Norman's in hospital?"

We never bought The Daily Sentinel. News spreads quicker through Middleville than chlamydia at an orgy. Dad's statement reminded me of that truth. I had only just learned that afternoon of Norman's 'accident' from his sister.

"Yeah. He's in a coma."

"Bike accident?"

"Something like that." My words sounded alien to me. "At the railway bridge."

Dad nodded. "Leon told me about it. But that's him. All headlines, sizzle and spark, but no meat or substance."

Despite the images of my best mate's quiet repose in the hospital bed lingering in my head, I laughed at Dad's estimation. Jeff, Leon's son, was the same. All story, but very little truth; it was like he told tales for the attention he attracted. Then thought of the machine that went beep next to Norman returned, and the smile faded from my face. "Yeah."

Dad may have been a council worker, but he used the six inches between his ears for more than head stuffing. "Something's not right."

"What do you mean?"

"Keith Mann says Norman took a tumble down the embankment from the hill. On his bike."

I offered a slow nod. "That's what the police told Norman's family."

One end of Dad's mouth stretched towards his ear. The smile he allowed when he noticed something wasn't genuine.

Silent, I waited for Dad's theory to emerge. "Norman had a part-time job at the town library, right?"

"Yep."

"So I understand why he rode up to the railway bridge. It's quicker than the old bridge and safer than Bueller Street. One passing truck can blow him and his bike off into the river. But when you ride up the dirt path to the railway bridge, there's only one way it can take you. Across the bridge, right?"

"We usually take the railway bridge, anyway," I agreed.

Dad paused a moment. The bridge is for pedestrians only. No bikes allowed. "Have you come close to falling down the embankment?"

I shook my head. "No. The path leads straight to the walkway. Even at full pedal power, he'd have slowed enough to stop falling over the edge."

Dad nodded, the wheels behind his eyes spinning. He had wondered the same as me. But would he make the next deduction?

"The police call it an accident, you say?"

"Yeah."

"Do you believe that?"

"They saw the broken vegetation where he and his bike rolled towards the river. He must have tumbled and injured his head on the way."

"I didn't ask what they saw, Robin." Dad's precision with language surprised most people who saw him in work overalls, which belies his education levels. He means what he states. "I asked if you believe it. Do you?"

I shook my head. "No, but I don't know everything that happened either."

"We won't until Norman wakes," my father responded. "He's the only one likely to tell us the truth." His tone softened a bit. "Do you want to talk about it?" I said nothing. "I mean, are you okay?"

"Yeah."

Dad stood there for a moment, his watchful eyes

scrutinising me. Sometimes he guessed my thoughts with uncanny accuracy. Other times, I reckon he bluffed me for the information. Somehow, I thought he was trying to trick me into saying something.

Ultimately, he turned and headed down the hall towards the kitchen. I released a breath..

No, I had no idea what had happened. But part of me guessed who happened. And that was before Maerie came onto the scene.

# CHAPTER 2

The strangest thoughts sat in my mind as I took the bus to the Mater Hospital the next day. Memories. Things like how we met, the trouble we got into together, and lots more. Norman had a big mouth for a skinny kid with glasses, and I was usually the one to get him out of fights.

Why these memories came, I don't know. But they came stronger when I saw him lying in the bed, motionless, his face still and limp in sleep. It was a private room -- his parents paid for it -- but the machines connected to him made it smaller. His mother and sister, Ella, were sitting beside him.

Norman's mother seemed the strongest woman to me. Confident in her movements and ability to know people, she posed a dominating force. At the Middleville Show, I'd seen her tell the attendant -- a Hell's Angel biker on holiday, I guess -- that he was cheating the kids. That was after Norman had lost money in a Defender video game that wasn't working. The showie claimed it was defective, and that someone had pulled tape off the coin slot, but he refused to give the money back. It was only forty cents, but Norman still told his Mum. She spoke loud enough for everyone around to turn heads with accusations of the biker was cheating kids of their money. I've never seen a man like a mountain turn to mush before. But he relinquished and returned Norman's money.

But, sitting beside Norman's bed, that tower of strength appeared a shadow of herself. A Womans Weekly magazine (Norman used to call it Menses because it comes out monthly, not weekly) sat on her lap, unopened and looking new. Bleary eyes, tinged with red fatigue, gazed at her son. I doubt she had slept the previous couple of days.

Both of them raised their eyes when I entered, alert to my

presence, but settled when they realised I wasn't a doctor. Mrs Cole managed a faint smile.

"Robin! We could have brought you here."

I shook my head. "It's okay, Mrs C."

She looked past me towards the door. "Where's your Dad?"

"I took the bus," I explained. "Dad said to pass on his wishes. He might come by on the weekend."

Ella offered me a smile above her paperback, a copy of Dean Koontz's Phantoms--a choice book, by my opinion. Although she looked equally exhausted, her youthful beauty outshone her apparent worry for her younger brother. Despite that, she remained the most beautiful girl in school to me, even if she was going out with some jerk.

Just as Mrs Cole rose to move, I stopped her. "There's another chair here."

The chair, one of those straight-backed metal frames with a vinyl-padded seat and back, was near the door. I carried it next to Norman and sat opposite his mother and sister.

The bandages round his head unsettled me. It's odd to realise that under the gauze wrappings my friend's brain jutted through a hole in his skull. Surgeons had removed a section to allow his swelling brain to protrude. Without it, he could have faced further brain damage. We don't like to think such things of our friends and loved ones. To witness their weaknesses or understand those biological things reminds us of our own mortality. And as a teenager, it's terrible to learn our perceived invincibility is a gaseous illusion.

Norman's face bore scratches from branches and stones from his fall. Yet his nose, its distinctive bridge like a ski jump, remained the same. But the bellows in the machine beside him that rose and fell with his breathing frightened the tar out of me.

For a long time, I sat there, shocked. My brain screamed, tortured by so many fears, and scrambled for ideas. What do I say? What do I do?

At last when I spoke, my voice fair startled his mother

and sister. "He knows we're here, right?"

Ella looked at me with mute surprise. Her eyes darted towards Mrs Cole who appeared as lost for words.

"I mean, like in the movies, can he hear us?"

They looked at each other. Then Mrs Cole shrugged. "They say he can. Would you like to say something?"

How awkward. Yeah, I wanted to talk to Norman. And I considered it. Maybe Ella and Mrs Cole said things. But how can you keep talking to someone who doesn't answer?

It felt strange to lean towards Norman's ear. "Hey, mate... Norman. It's Robbo here." Nothing happened. What did I expect, a fluttering of Norman's eyelids and his head turning towards me? "I guess you can hear me. You don't have to say anything back. I want you to know I'm here."

In the corner, the brain wave detector machine kept recording Norman's brain function with a fluctuation cycle. I knew it wasn't the ECG because that measures heart rates. The little stylus in its printer scribbled back and forth like a mad two-year-old, but no great changes happened. Nothing to convince me that Norman heard me. If Norman perceived me in that blackness between his ears, he wasn't responding-- or couldn't.

Ella shifted. My gazed flicked towards her. How long had she tried talking to Norman before tiring? As his eider sister, she often tormented him when we were younger. Sometimes siblings tease or shout or fight so much that it's hard to tell how much they love each other. Until something shakes them back to reality. But now in the hospital, she looked weary, her eyes outlined by concern and worry.

But I didn't want to give up on my mate. I kept talking.

"Mate, wake up soon, will you? The Golden Child starts next week at the pictures. I don't want to go alone."

If Norman were awake, he would have laughed. Maybe he would have said something else like Oh, you mean you need a wing-man.

That would have made us both laugh hard because he was the one most awkward round girls. And we both knew the cinema is a rubbish place to pick up girlfriends. That and the library. And bowling.

I remember glancing at Ella when I mentioned the cinema. She pretended not to care what I said, but my blush still warmed my face and ears. Then I focused on my friend's inert body again.

Part of me wanted to make a smart-arse comment like asking Norman if he needed training wheels. He might have given me the finger for that, if he could, but I doubted his mother would appreciate it.

So many inappropriate things flashed across my mind, none of which I could say then. So I filtered them. Before long I realised I had little to say and understood why Ella and Mrs Cole sat there like those silent statues reading books on park benches. It was all they could do.

"Ella." Her name caught in my throat, and I almost choked again when she looked up at me. "You must be -" Why was it so hard to talk to her? "- getting ready for year 12 now."

Smooth as a lame horse's hide, Robin.

Ella's face clouded, turned a slight pink, and her eyes flicked towards her mother who shifted subtly. "No." An uncomfortable silence of only two seconds swept the room. "I'm repeating year eleven."

Repeating? Just like I repeated first grade.

She looked at her mother again, and I realised what must have happened. Ella hadn't passed with high enough grades. I found that hard to believe, but I also knew what taskmasters Norman and Ella's parents could be--especially Mr Cole.

An uncomfortable pause came over us, and I turned towards Norman, unsure what to say. As Norman's best friend, I sure had a way of making things uncomfortable for his folks. And I probably looked like a bigger dork to Ella.

But I opened my mouth, anyway.

"That's not as bad as repeating first grade." Ella and Mrs Cole both looked at me, mixed thoughts in their eyes. "I missed most of it the first time. Had tonsillitis." Ella's look of thunder softened. "That's what my father said, anyway. I think it's because I refused to colour between the lines." I winked and Mrs Cole chuckled, while Ella allowed herself to smile. "That's how I first met Norman."

Mrs Cole's face lit with recognition. "I didn't realise you had repeated. I always thought you were a big boy compared to Norman. You protected him from the bullies."

The warm blush filled my face to my throat. "Yeah. They used to be friends of mine before that."

Then I remembered. One of those bullies was Ella's boyfriend. That same group of jerks had picked on Norman right until the last day of grade ten.

My eyes flicked towards Ella. My wise crack about grade one had lightened her expression now I'd deflected attention from her repeating eleventh grade. How could someone so attractive let herself go out with a jerk who picked on her brother? "How's Johnno doing?" Not that I cared, but it produced a smile again, even if it was about him. That was my plan, but it didn't happen.

Ella's hand twitched. With the hint of a vacant look, she rubbed her back. "He's okay." Her voice changed.

Did her eyes flick towards her mother? I couldn't tell. Mrs Cole, whose gaze remained on Norman, appeared not to notice. Then they lifted, looked past me.

I turned to see what had caught her attention.

There she was. A girl about my age I didn't recognise.

Hair, black as a raven's feathers, hung to her shoulders. Despite their soft dark brown hue, her eyes looked hard at us as she stood at the door. An involuntary shiver shuddered through my body.

Behind me, the stylus quickened its pace on the machine like a furious kid colouring paper as it beeped. Dark lines appeared on the paper that spat and spilled to the floor. Three sheets later, it slowed to its normal pace.

I remembered and glanced towards the girl.

But she was gone.

# CHAPTER 3

Wednesday, I rode to the school, which is a weird thing to do on school holidays. I'd finished grade ten, the new school year didn't start until the end of January. The bike racks were full because the lower grades still had a fortnight to go before finishing. But I had to be there to pick up my Junior Certificate, the piece of paper that said we'd finished grade ten. The teachers told us of its value in finding a job, but I don't know. To me, it only said how well we read books and passed in school. It never reflects our true passions, how good we were, nor our ability to think independently. Years later, I believe that even more. I can't speak for anyone who finished school at Year 10, but I can't say that Junior Certificate--or any other report - ever helped me win a job.

There were others ahead of me in line when I reached the school office: a mixture of students and parents. And there was only one queue, which snaked its way back downstairs to the drinking taps.

I wished I'd brought a novel to read. Unabridged.

In the line ahead of me stood Randall Seppings. I remembered his father as one of the local electricians who lived three-or-four blocks from my place. He glanced at me, his bored expression changing upon recognising me, and nodded. "This is the last line I'm standing in here." A grin flashed from his freckled face as he rolled his eyes at the line's length.

"Not coming back?"

He shook his head. "Going for an apprenticeship."

"With your Dad?"

"Nope. Plumbing." Randall never showed his enthusiasm for anything in school if it didn't involve football. But this time, his teeth shone in an ear-to-ear grin. He bobbed his head towards the other students. "Everyone here will need their pipes fixed some time." I considered plumbing to be a shitty job but said nothing. "Hey, I hear Norman Cole's in hospital."

Randall knew Norman and I to be mates. He wanted gossip.

I nodded. "In a coma."

He looked at the line ahead of us and directed my gaze to a few noisier students. The same guys who had bullied Norman a few weeks earlier. "I overheard those jerk-offs talking about it. Not sure if they're talking shit, but part of me wonders how they know so much."

"Like what?"

"How he flipped over the handlebars under the bridge and hit his head."

"Under the bridge?" The words left my mouth before I could stop them. "Which one?"

Randall shrugged. "I didn't hear. Stubbs turned up and the conversation changed."

I looked past Randall towards the others and saw Matthew Stubbs with some of the others. In the past, I always wondered who the real ringleader was out of that group. Stubbs' father owned a bunch of stores across town. At least, they started as stores but changed to those little shopping centre blocks that include medical centres and newsagencies. I could see him as the leader. But then there was Richard Crane whose father was a cop and always carried himself as though he held authority. The others - Jason Baker, Louis Patch, Paul Thornton and John O'Sullivan - were a curious bunch. Sometimes, they were followers; at others, eager participants.

John was the only one who seemed different because he was Ella's boyfriend. I considered him two-faced because he was going out with Norman's sister while associating himself with the bullies. Maybe the association came through their football team. Maybe the cricket. But whatever it was, I didn't know what Ella saw in John.

A funny feeling crept over me and prompted me to ask.

"What else did they say?"

Randall shrugged. "Something about how he went arse-over-apex over the handlebars when his front wheel stopped." Randall looked like he could say more words when his gaze shifted. "Here's his sister now."

I turned in time to see Ella reach the end of the line, ten people behind me. A gallant idea crossed my mind, and nervousness rushed to stop it at the pass. Should I call out to Ella to jump in the queue with me? No, said my nervous side. Reason stepped in to save the day.

I waved to catch Ella's attention. On the second wave, she saw me and, with a grateful smile, left the end of the line and stood next to me. "Thanks," she said. I offered a smile I hoped didn't appear too shy and dorky. A few others behind us grumbled, but I didn't care. She stepped in next to me. It felt good, damned good, and wow! My heart raced.

A noise ahead in the line distracted us. Matthew Stubbs' was laughing at something Richard Crane must have said. They were busy yapping to each other. Ella took a small step around me until she stood out of the direct vision. But I thought she was friends with them too.

An inner voice suggested I say something. "Are you here for Norman's certificate?"

Ella glanced ahead in the line again and back to me. "Yeah. Mum's at the hospital now."

The line started to move, and we took a few steps before it stopped again. "What about you? Are you going up later?"

She nodded, and I glimpsed her eyes, blue as the water in a Gold Coast postcard. "Probably. I -"

"Yo! Ella!"

We looked towards the voice. Matthew Stubbs was looking at us. "Come on down here, Ella."

Ella shook her head at him and faced me again. "I wanted a break from the hospital."

"Ella!" Louis Patch's voice. "What are you doing here, anyway?"

Matthew Stubbs punched Louis' shoulder. "Why do you

think she's here? Norman's in hospital. Remember?"

Remember?

What did that mean? Yes, some from school knew, but the way he said it caught my ear.

Louis was slow sometimes, enough to make Middleville's bus service seem punctual. "Yeah, I-"

Matthew punched Louis' shoulder again to stop him talking.

I glanced towards Ella, but her expression betrayed nothing. Had she heard? Or did my resentment towards Norman's bullies colour my perceptions?

When I faced front again, Matthew was already next to me. The way he looked at Ella, features softened to apparent sympathy, made me want to puke. Ever since he was in second grade, the year I repeated first grade, I'd recognised his tactic of being an arse-kisser. Now he used his connection with John--Ella's boyfriend — to deceive her too. "Ella," his voice was even and caring, "come up here with us. You can go home sooner and back to the hospital."

I noticed he didn't ask about Norman.

Randall feigned disinterest, affording only a short glance or two, but I knew what ticked behind his quiet eyes. Ella's eyes flicked between Matthew, his friends ahead of us in line, and me. I wanted to tell them to bugger off. But I had no rational reason. I thrilled at being with her and detested the thought of Ella hanging out with Matthew. And part of me knew Matthew wanted to get in her pants. His butter-wouldn't-melt-in-my-mouth act couldn't disguise it enough for me.

"Come on, Ella." With his face lowered to her level, he worked his voice like a pro. "You want to get back to Norman, don't you?"

Ella's hesitation was all I needed.

"Matthew, how about you leave her alone?"

Fire flashed in his eyes for a moment. He straightened to his full five foot ten with his chest puffed. I stood taller too, one inch higher. "All I want to do is help."

"Were you the one who pressed the button when your mates flushed his head in the toilet six months ago?" I asked.

A laugh escaped from Louis Patch's mouth. Matthew shot him a withering glance before confronting me again. "That was six months ago. This is now."

"Wasn't it ten minutes ago that I heard Louis, Jason, and you laughing about Norman's accident?" Randall's voice surprised me, but it floored Matthew and Louis enough to drain the colour from their faces.

Matthew swallowed hard and his Adams apple bobbed somewhere in his thick neck. Randall stood taller than Matthew, too, and we knew Randall could fight--and hit hard. Matthew's lips moved without a sound.

"Pardon?" Randall's voice was soft but carried punch. "Did you say something?"

Matthew glanced at Louis who was stepping back to where Jason stood in line. "No. I don't know what you mean. I just want to-"

"Yeah, sure. You said you want to help, but let Ella speak for herself." I turned to Ella whose eyes looked hardened, a dangerous blend of blue flame mixed with anger.

"No, Matthew. I'm happy standing here with Rob and Randall. Thank you."

Matthew hesitated, wheels turning behind his eyes as he considered his words. "Okay. Do you need anything?"

"Yes, Matthew," Ella replied. "I need genuine friends."

"But-"

"Butt out."

Matthew's eyes flicked towards the growing number of people in the queue--including some parents--who were watching the whole thing. Common sense, or maybe self-preservation for his family name and reputation, kicked in. "Okay, Ella, no problem." He took a step away. "Let me know if you need anything, right?"

Ella didn't reply. Matthew glanced at Randall, then at me, and I saw a glimmer of hatred darken his features before he turned on his heel and returned to his friends.

A breath I didn't realise I'd been holding escaped. Amusement showed on Randall's face as he looked at Ella. "Good one, Ella," he said.

She smiled back at Randall and me. "I've been an idiot, haven't I?"

"What do you mean?"

"For going out with John who is friends with Norman's bullies."

Randall and I looked at each other, knowing John had done things too, but said nothing. Some things aren't worth saying.

"You're lucky," Randall said. "I could end up cleaning their shit from their clogged dunnies."

The rest of the wait in line passed quicker. Conversation can do that, and Randall provided us with the laughs until we reached the front desk and collected our certificates. We let Ella collect Norman's certificate first, so she left before us. Randall soon collected his, and it was my turn. The secretary flicked through the envelopes in search of my name. "Robert?" she asked.

I shook my head. "Robin. Like the bird."

A quizzical look crossed her face as she checked another long list. "But you already have yours."

"No, I don't."

The secretary turned around a folder and pointed to something on the sheet. "Is that your name?" Sure enough, it was my name. Next to it was a red tick. "It's ticked because you collected it."

I shook my head. "Nope. Couldn't have. I've been in line the whole time."

From the other end of the old building, a laugh echoed. Louis. The sound of paper tearing and crumpling. The plop of something in an empty metal bin's bottom.

"I never had it." But I knew who did.

The secretary's eyebrow rose, mixed scepticism and doubt written on her face as she studied me. At last, she decided. "I'll make another one for you."

Fifteen minutes later, I had another copy signed fresh for me. They even put it in a crisp white envelope for me, which I slid into my backpack before returning to the bike racks.

But the relief soon washed away when I reached the bike racks. Two slashed tyres gaped, the slashes forming toothless mouths, at me from my bike.

Matthew and his mates couldn't beat me with words or fists, but he could still make life difficult.

# CHAPTER 4

I'm not sure who slashed my tyres--Matthew or Louis. But they knew how to get under my skin. I refused to satisfy their sadism by ranting or raving either. With their laughs still echoing in my memory, it took me the better part of an hour to walk my bike home. The kitchen clock's little hand was just passing the eleven when I arrived, sweaty and my head aching from the heat.

It could have been worse. By chance, two spare tubes sat in boxes in the cool shade under the house; but I still needed two new tyres. Another three-quarters of an hour later, I was back from Kmart--a short walk from home--with my new tyres.

By one o'clock, I'd finished repairs, had lunch and cleaned myself ready to visit Norman in hospital. Stuffed from the morning's activity, I opted to take the bus. Besides, it was the middle of a hot summer's day.

At a little after two o'clock, I moseyed into Norman's room at the Mater. There sat Mrs Cole and Ella.

"Sorry, I'm late," I said, for Ella's benefit. "Something came up."

"That's okay." Mrs Cole offered a smile. "You missed nothing. We were just talking to Norman about his marks on his certificate." I knew Mrs Cole would miss my meaning, but Ella raised an eyebrow. I nodded with a smile to let her know all was well.

Meanwhile, Mrs Cole was telling me about Norman's grades which were lower than he expected. Why was that? She knew he didn't have a girlfriend. In fact, Norman had been visiting the library on Norseman Street more. Why, she didn't know. Things were quiet enough at home to study without him riding halfway across North Middleville. From my perspective, I couldn't tell her much. As far as I knew,

Norman's grades were fine. He might have slipped from scoring ninety-eight to one-hundred percent to ninety-five percent. But so what? From my eighty-six percent levels, his grades were awesome. I felt sorry for Norman. Even in a coma, he couldn't escape his domineering mother arse-aching about a drop in grades--even if he was still earning a B-plus or A-minus average!

I whispered to Norman as I reached into my backpack. "It's okay, mate. I brought just the thing for you."

"What's that?" Mrs Cole asked, a defensive tone in her voice.

"Headphones and my Walkman," I replied, slipping them over his ears. "I thought Norman might enjoy listening to some music."

I pressed Play and adjusted the volume for Norman's ears, not wanting to blow the poor guy's eardrums out. No way did I want him waking later and bitching about being deaf.

Mrs Cole bristled. "He was doing fine listening to us."

Norman might not have complained, but neither could he say anything. But I couldn't tell Mrs Cole that. The shock of her son's accident and condition had blown away Mrs Cole's possessiveness over Norman, but her domineering nature was returning to full strength. I was used to standing up to her, but it wasn't the place--far better to grease the rails for Norman's sake this time. "Just a change in pace for him."

After a few seconds of song-play, heard only by Norman's ears, the ECG machine kicked into overdrive and spewed inky paper from its thin mouth. Again? Sensing Mrs Cole's mood shifting, I was about to press the Stop button when a voice interrupted.

"Let it play. Norman likes that song." The voice from the doorway surprised Mrs Cole who was about to give me a retort. "Especially that song."

I turned towards the door and almost dropped the Walkman in surprise. It was the girl I'd seen the day before.

"That one?" I asked, wondering how good the girl's ears

were. Yes, one poked out from her dark hair, like an elf's ear might look but sexier.

She looked at me, regarded me with a knowing gaze, and approached. "Yes. That's Glory of Love by Peter Cetera, isn't it?"

She was right. "How did you know that?" I'd only made the tape for Norman the previous night. When Norman and I had seen the movie at the cinema on the September holidays, he had sung that song heaps, taking the mickey out of it.

The girl reached Norman, and something about her made me step back as she placed her hand on his. The way she touched him was alien. It wasn't just a touch, the kind a friend might do, for she caressed it in the way a lover might. Prickles rose across my neck as waves of goose pimples washed across my arms and legs.

"Who are you?" Mrs Cole's voice was direct, yet curious.

The mystery girl remained silent, regarding Norman's face with compassionate eyes. At last, she looked up. At that moment, the medical machine lit up like a Christmas tree, but the printer's plotting slowed to its former steady pace.

"He knows I'm here." She looked at me. "Glory of Love is our song. It was playing on the radio when we first met." Then she turned to Mrs Cole. "You must be Norman's mother. My name is Maerie." She pronounced it as may-ri.

Mrs Cole's mouth dropped. "Maerie?" She looked at Ella who reflected her surprise and shrugged. After a second, Mrs Cole found her voice again. "I'm sorry, dear, but I don't remember Norman mentioning you.

"I understand." Maerie glanced at Norman, then at Mrs Cole, before looking at me. She glanced away, and I guessed what she wanted but didn't ask. Standing, I motioned towards my seat, which the strange girl took with no acknowledgement while I found another on which to sit. "Norman was reluctant to tell you straight away about me."

A surprised expression crossed Mrs Cole's face, or maybe shock. One thing Norman copped flack about at school was his mother's possessive hold over him. At one particular time in fourth grade, Norman had forgotten his lunch. It didn't bother him until his mother appeared at the classroom door, covered in make-up and dressed prim-and-proper, gave him his lunchbox, and kissed his cheek so he glowed an embarrassed red. A redder lipstick mark stood in darker contrast. Word soon reached the bullies in the higher grades who never let him recover from the incident.

"I don't know what you mean." Mrs Cole sniffed. "Norman and I have a very close relationship. He keeps nothing from me."

A smile flicked at the corner of Maerie's mouth. "Yet you're surprised at his wishes."

"How do you know Norman?" The same intrigue filled my mind as Norman's mother expressed. But I added, "I'm Robin."

Maerie regarded me with beaming eyes. "I thought so. Norman talks about you a lot. He never told you about me, it seems. I'm sure he wanted to; boys are like girls and like to tell their best friends, but maybe he wasn't ready yet."

"I guess so," I said, "but that doesn't matter. Where did you meet?"

"The library on Norseman Street." So specific. "It was in the last four weeks. We were both studying there."

The answer to Mrs Cole's conundrum was plain. Norman had been studying, but he had another interest.

"His grades weren't their usual high standard." Mrs Cole's voice could have withered flowers at ten paces. "You're the reason he was failing."

An unfazed Maerie laughed. "Oh, we studied, Mrs Cole. And his understanding improved a lot. But I have a question. Why aren't you happy for your son's happiness in finding someone he loves and trusts?"

Ella leaned across Norman towards Maerie with an outstretched hand. "I'm Ella. Norman's sister." She allowed a glance at her mother. "Mum's just surprised to learn something about my brother that none of us knew."

Mrs Cole sniffed and regarded Maerie a moment. "That's true. You're not what I expected Norman to -" Ella tried to interrupt, but Maerie spoke first.

"Norman is a better gentleman than my parents expected of me."

That gave Norman's mother reason to pause. "Gentleman?" Her features softened. "Of course, he's a gentleman. Perhaps that's the real reason he never told me about you."

For a moment, I wondered. Did Ella's boyfriend face a similar grilling? I gazed at Ella as I wondered and imagined that scene.

Ella's hand rested on her mother's arm to calm her. "Maerie, we're sorry. You're Norman's first girlfriend (she hesitated using that word) and the accident..."

Maerie nodded her understanding. "It's been a shock. Perhaps I should have come another time. It's just that my mother has someone else to care for her today, and I -"

Norman's mother's eyebrows lifted. "You care for your mother? Is she -?"

Maerie shook her head. "You need not hear about my mother's problems, Mrs Cole. If you want me to leave (she stood) then I can return another time." She turned to leave, and Mrs Cole stopped her.

"Please. Stay."

Something flickered on the mystery girl's face. The hint of a smile? I couldn't tell. And she faced Mrs Cole again. "Are you sure?"

"Yes, dear, I am." Mrs Cole stood, a smile crossing her face that signalled recognition of her son's girlfriend's value. Value for her, more than for her son. "I apologise for my tone. Perhaps we can start fresh?" She walked around Norman's bed towards Maerie with outstretched hand. "You can call me Ruth."

Maerie shook Mrs Cole's hand. "Thank you, Mrs Cole. I'm Maerie. I am new to Middleville too."

"Where do you come from?"

Maerie's eyes flicked. "Melbourne. We came here for the warmer weather."

Mrs Cole smile, fanning herself. "That, we have."

A breath I didn't realise waited inside me escaped as the room's tension eased. Pleasantries passed back and forth, and as I listened, I realised something. Mrs Cole's usual attempts to manipulate conversations and feelings didn't work on Maerie. The girl was stronger than she appeared. And as the conversation continued, my curiosity in Maerie grew. Even Ella asked questions, leaning forward, and hung on Maerie's every word.

At last, Mrs Cole asked. "How did you know Norman was here?"

Maerie's eyes gazed at Norman's face, placid in comatose sleep. "He wasn't at the library on Monday."

Mrs Cole's head tilted to the side as she waited. But Maerie gave no further answer. The silence felt awkward.

"Who told you he was here?"

No answer. She didn't even break her gaze. It was as if she was staring into Norman's skull and at his brain to find whatever kept him sleeping. Even Mrs Cole and Ella shifted in their seats as though trying to fill the silent void.

At last, she looked up from Norman. It was like nothing had happened, and she turned to me. "I asked around." Then she resumed gazing at Norman.

Asked around? Middleville may be a gossip mill, but with a 76,000 population, that would still take a lot of asking if you're new to town.

Then she looked at me, cutting the uncomfortable silence as she said, "Norman mentioned a name to me once. Louis Patch?"

"How did his name come up?" I asked. Already my mind flipped to the morning's recent events. What had Norman said about one of his lifelong tormentors?

Maerie's eyes flicked towards Ella, mine did too, enough to see Ella's face turn pale, and back to me. Did her eye sparkle a moment as she stared at me? Or did my vision shift? I blinked. Perhaps walking in the hot sun earlier affect my head. As soon as the dizziness started, it subsided like the tides.

Then she shook her head. "It's nothing. Just one of those things that came up."

An unsettling wave of wooziness hit again.

"Is everything okay?" Mrs Cole asked. "You look like you're ready to faint."

Rubbing my temples, I blinked a few times, nodding to let her know all was well. "Just a touch of the sun this morning."

Someone moved. The rustle of a newspaper. Fabric sounds. A feminine movement. But I couldn't see through the greying vision. Then it cleared again. A hand rested on my shoulder. Motherly. Norman's mother.

I nodded, shook my head, and looked around. Ella and Mrs Cole were beside me. Besides them, it was only Norman and I in the room.

"Where's Maerie?"

"She's gone to get you something to drink." Mrs Cole looked at the clock on the wall. "I'd better go and check. Ella, stay here with Robin and Norman. I'll be right back. The girl probably went to the canteen instead of the water fountain."

With that, she left too.

And I was alone.

With the girl for whom I held a crush.

Ella.

Perhaps I wasn't so alone. Norman was there, too, asleep and all.

"What happened in the sun?" Ella asked, sitting next to me.

I shook my head. "I had a flat tyre. Had to walk the bike home from school."

Ella's voice sounded like her head was in two places. "Oh."

A yawn escaped my mouth. "Probably tired from walking in the sun. That's all."

Ella's closeness conjured thrills through my skin. She was a ruler's length away from me, but this was the first time I'd been alone with her. And many things came to my attention. Her smell. The lightness of her voice. The thought of holding her hand. My eye flicked to the skin above her bare knees. But Norman was there too. It didn't feel right.

"What do you think Maerie meant when she asked about Louis?" she asked.

I looked at Ella. Didn't she know?

"Louis bullied Norman a lot through grade nine and this year," I said, watching her face as I answered. "Didn't he tell you?"

Ella's eyebrows raised in surprise. "Bullied? But that stopped after a couple of years ago."

She didn't know, or didn't want to, and I guessed her time with John O'Sullivan did that.

"Louis, Matthew, and the others picked on Norman all the time," I explained. "High school has been a shit of a time for your brother." A guilty feeling swept across me. "And because I have some classes different to him, I can't always be there to look out for him."

Ella shifted, her leg closest to me crossing away from me. "I don't believe it."

I took a breath, wishing we could have talked about something else.

Louis had been the worst bully for Norman--the most physical. Grade nine was the worst time. At one time in particular, Louis had cornered Norman in the manual arts woodwork class. That was a class I shared with Norman, but I wasn't there that day because I was away sick. Norman told me on the Saturday when he visited my place. Louis, he said, had waited for the teacher to leave the class before bumping into Norman who was wood planing his project then. He kept pushing Norman around. At first, they were light pushes while he jibed Norman. Soon he shoved harder. One fellow told Louis to settle, leave Norman alone, but it did no good. Norman felt small, alone, abandoned. The next thing

Norman knew was the cold steel at his throat. A chisel. Louis Patch's voice hissing in his ear. The growing wet patch on his pants that ran from his shorts down his leg. He thought he was going to die. The teacher arrived in time though. Patch left school for six months. He told everyone it was for a correspondence school. But we knew the real reason. The school had suspended Patch for six months. Upon his return, although more subdued, Louis still let Norman know he was around.

"Louis hasn't bothered Norman all year."

I shook my head. "He kept pushing his weight with Norman. Maybe Norman never told you, but I heard all about it."

I hated telling her that, but no way was I letting my hots for Ella get in the way. Norman would owe me big for that favour if he ever woke.

Ella turned quiet with something jumping through her thoughts and waving through her eyes at me. "What's Maerie want with Louis?"

I shrugged. Then upon remembering the way I felt before she left. The creepy feeling across my head like someone was looking through my thoughts. I shuddered.

Perhaps that's how I knew before it happened.

# CHAPTER 5

That night I dreamt I was on the old bridge at Boundary Road that crosses Grants Creek. The street lights, distant between each other, did little to illuminate the darkness. Yet I could see something not right. A young couple near where the creek met the Fitzroy River. They seemed to be playing together in the darkness, the way lovers do in movies. Silhouetted in the moonlight, their features remained unclear. A laugh. She darted from him, but he feinted and caught her. Another laugh, feminine. They held each other, standing. Mixed with dread came a guilty, yet voyeuristic, pleasure that scared me. I woke with sweat pouring from my forehead in the summer air, my arousal thankfully not manifested. I checked my shorts. Nope. Lucky. I didn't want the self-conscious trip past the living room where I could hear Dad watching some movie in the small hours. So far, I hadn't admitted having wet dreams — and I didn't want to explain any that night either. What bothered me most was the guy resembled Louis Patch. The girl, though familiar, I didn't know.

Sleep returned, but not straight away.

At about seven, I woke and dragged myself out of bed. A few images still remained in my head. Tiredness clung to me like the smell of wet dog on a blanket. So after eating my cereal, I lazed on the living room couch to read some Phantom comics. At about eight, a knock on the door interrupted me.

The sound of the shower spraying told me Dad was awake, but busy. So I answered the door. There stood a policeman with a large muscled frame that threatened to pop his shirt's buttons and seams, and a droopy moustache.

"Are you Robert Mitchell?"

"Robin," I corrected him, my mouth dry.

"Do you know Louis Patch?"

I nodded, aware then of another officer standing at the bottom of the front stairs. "From school."

"We need to ask you some questions."

I stood aside to allow them in, but he stayed there.

"At the station."

My heart stopped. A dangerous and deadly darkness sat behind his voice. "Why?"

"We need to question you about Louis Patch."

A lump grew in my stomach, churning my insides. Flashes of last night's dreams flickered in my head. I hesitated, not knowing what to do.

"Come along, Mr Mitchell." He reached forward to place his hand on my shoulder.

"Stay where you are, Robin." My father's voice, deep and calm, sent momentary relief through me. I hadn't heard him approach from the hallway. His hair wet from the shower as he stood there in his work pants and singlet, Dad eyed the copper hard. "What do you want from my son... David?"

The policeman, who I later learned to be Richard Crane's father, didn't falter. He glared back at Dad. "We need to question Robin about Louis Patch, Gary." His gaze turned to me. "Did you have an altercation with Louis yesterday?"

I opened my mouth but Dad's hand stopped me.

"Why?"

"Louis Patch's body was found this morning, Gary. We heard from a witness of a confrontation between Robin and Louis yesterday morning."

Dad looked at me, a hint of concern peeking from behind his placid features. For three heartbeats, he studied me then offered a brief smile. "Grab your shoes. But don't say a thing until I arrive with your aunt."

Don't say a thing.

That was hard advice to follow. What could I say that would land me in trouble? Probably anything, I figured.

So I took my first trip in the back of a police car, looking through the wire grille at the front window. The seats smelled like urine; maybe I'd meet the pisser in the watch-house. Worst of all, the officer driving the car travelled slower than the speed limit, which made the trip longer. Whenever we passed anyone who knew me, I shrunk back from view and wished the car went quicker. At last, we reached the police station on Reagan Street where they took me to a little room with a table and two chairs. There I sat... and waited.

Time dragged. Without my watch, I could only guess how much time passed - maybe half an hour - before a detective entered through the door, shutting it behind him before sitting opposite me. The manilla folder he held plopped on the wooden table, and he gazed at me a moment before speaking.

"Robert Mitchell?"

"Robin."

"Robin?" He regarded me with a stupid look, the kind one has when sitting on a cream pie, and opened the file to read something. "As in Batman and Robin?" His finger moved over the first typewritten page until he found something. "Yes, of course." Then he looked at me.

I said nothing, just waited with a hammering heart and racing mind. Another detective entered, shut the door, and waited in the corner behind me. What a trapped feeling.

Then the seated detective turned on a tape recorder, said aloud the date and time, and began. "Can you confirm your name and address?"

I replied.

"Do you understand what you say can and will be used against you?"

Just like a TV show. I was about to answer when I remembered Dad's warning: say nothing until he arrived with my aunt.

I answered with silence.

"Can you answer the question please?"

"I'm saying nothing."

With a sigh, the detective shook his head. "We need to

ask you questions about Louis Patch. It will be easier for you to answer now, rather than later." His words landed heavy, which I'm sure he intended.

I shrugged.

This kept up back and forth, my stonewalling every time, until a knock on the door interrupted. The second detective moved to the door, while my interrogator turned off the tape recorder. I looked up and smiled upon recognising the new person at the door. My aunty Deb.

Dressed in her familiar royal-blue dress and her hair styled to perfection, she bustled into the room. A smile flickered on her mouth upon seeing me before she regarded the detective who sat opposite me. "I'm Robin's solicitor and representative. Do you realise he's a minor?"

The detective sitting opposite me sighed with recognition. "Yes, and he has said nothing more than his name and address."

Aunty Deb regarded me with another brief smile, her eyes watchful just like Dad's. "You don't have to say anything more, Robin." She looked at the second detective. "Chair, please."

He bustled away to retrieve it.

"Why is Robin here?"

"We are questioning him in relation to a homicide."

If it shocked my aunt, she didn't show it. "Is he being charged or under arrest?"

Detective Crane sighed. "Just questioning."

Aunty Deb cast a withering gaze. "Yet you have the boy in an interrogation room. Couldn't you question him at his home, Detective Crane?"

Surprised, I studied the detective. Could it be? Yes, I saw the family resemblance. His son Richard was a friend of Louis Patch. And Matthew Stubbs.

The second detective arrived with a chair for Aunty Deb, placing it for her before resuming his position behind me.

Aunty Deb turned to me. "Robin. The police will ask you questions. Remember you don't have to answer everything."

She smiled, squeezing my hand.

Detective Crane's eyes narrowed at me for a moment. Starting the tape recorder again, he re-stated the date and time, asked me my name and address, and we continued.

"Did you see Louis Patch yesterday?"

I nodded.

"Answer for the recorder, please."

"Yes."

"What happened?"

"Nothing much. He and Matthew Stubbs spoke with my friend Ella. She wanted nothing to do with them, and they persisted in asking her to stand with them in line. So me and someone else told them to leave Ella alone."

Detective Crane paused. "What about your bike?"

Yes, I could see what happened now, but the question confused me. I hesitated.

"Did something happen to your bike?"

"How is this relevant?" Aunty Deb demanded.

He maintained his focus on me. "Just gathering facts. Can you answer the question, Robin?"

I shrugged. "Someone slashed my tyres. I had to walk."

"Did you see Louis Patch again after that?"

An image flashed across my mind from the dream. I heard Patch's voice and the girl's cheeky laugh. Perhaps I waited too long; he repeated his question and I shook my head. "No."

A sceptical look crossed his face as his eyes burrowed into my head, watching, thinking. The clock above the door ticked away three or four seconds.

"Where were you last night between 10pm and 5am?

The dream memory returned. Stronger. "Home. Asleep."

"Can anyone verify that?"

"My father would have arrived home at about ten-thirty."

Aunty Deb interrupted. "Where is this leading?"

But Detective Crane ignored her. "Did you want payback for your tyres being slashed?"

Shock filled me. "No! They're just tyres, and I don't know

who did it." Although I had a good idea, that was true.

Aunty Deb's hand on my shoulder calmed me. "Relax, Robin. Detective Crane has finished his questions now." Then she glared at him. "Unless he wants to charge you for defending a girl."

Detective Crane shook his head. "I have no further questions. You're not being charged."

Aunty Deb looked long and hard at Crane. "You questioned my client based upon something less than a schoolyard scrap. Circumstantial evidence. Having known you so long, I expect better, Jeff. I'm disappointed." Disappointment appeared in her eyes, and Detective Crane bowed his head for a moment like a little boy who has done wrong.

Before I could wonder more, Aunty Deb stood. "Come on, Rob. You're supposed to be enjoying your holidays."

Crane hurried to open the door for us. I don't know what expression his face had, but he was quiet, and I didn't dare look as we quit the room.

Meanwhile, recollection of the dream came to mind stronger, so I didn't notice the hot, bright sun as we left the building. Aunty Deb might have said something to me. Maybe Dad did too. But if I heard, I didn't listen. The dream vision hung in my thoughts too hard.

Why did I dream of Louis the night he died?

# CHAPTER 6

The fears I held of Dad judging me for the morning's events soon disappeared on the way home. Aunty Deb who sat in the front seat told Dad about what happened in the interrogation (interviewing) room. Then, his voice calm as always, Dad asked me about the previous day. I told him and left out nothing.

If he had known about it before, he didn't say. Middleville's gossip mill was fast but didn't always include schoolyard events.

When I finished, he merely kept his eye on the road until we dropped off Aunty Deb at her place. Away from the police station, her tone had softened to the familiar Aunty Deb, Dad's sister. She turned in the front seat to look back at me.

"Don't worry about the police. Detective Crane is a good man."

"You sure chewed him out though."

She allowed a brief smile. "He needed pulling into line. If anything else comes up, let me know." She winked. "See ya, Rob," she called through my open window as the car moved away.

"What did she mean by that?" I asked Dad as he drove us home. "The part about pulling into line."

"A bit of history there," he replied, slowing to check traffic before crossing the intersection. "Your Aunty Deb used to go out with Jeff Crane in high school days. That was before she went to college to learn law."

"What happened?"

"He met another girl and married her." His tone changed, lifting a bit. "How about some fishing today?"

"Fishing?" I said, thinking about Dad. "Shouldn't you be at work?"

He glanced at me through the rear-view mirror. "Let's talk."

"About what?"

"Louis Patch. Didn't you used to be friends with him?"

I shook my head at the notion. "Not since he went off the rails after his brother died in the accident in '82. It was too hard talking to him without his wanting to pick a fight."

Dad was silent. I could almost guess his thoughts. Louis was now with his brother - maybe. Then he said, "I guess he felt the world owed him something. Maybe he's feeling better now."

The words prickled anger within me, which I suppressed. Dad wasn't on Louis' side; he was showing compassion. Soon we arrived home, grabbed our fishing gear, and hooked up the dinghy to his Toyota Landcruiser. Then we were off to the Fitzroy River's boat ramp near the "old bridge", stopping only to buy some grub from the shop on the corner of Teal and Main Streets.

We were just putting the dinghy in the water when I noticed a movement among the shady trees. With my hand shading my eyes from the blinding sun, I peered and saw Darren Butler. I hadn't seen Darren since we finished seventh grade. He went to Middleville High, a different high school to me, but we still saw each other on the odd occasion. This was the oddest.

I lifted a hand in greeting, and his white teeth flashed from the shadows in contrast to his dark skin. "Yo! Darren!"

In one hand he held his fishing rod. The other gripped an empty toy wagon which I assume he used for keeping his catch. He must have just arrived. We slapped palms, laying some skin. "Robin! How you doin', brother?"

"Not bad," I replied. "Yourself?"

"Trying to stay out of trouble." He flashed another grin, the kind no one could resist. "I hear you were at the cop shop, mate."

My jaw dropped. News sure spread faster than AIDS at an orgy here. "That was quick. Who told you?"

He laughed, slapping my shoulder. "I saw you in the back of the police car when it passed my house. What happened?"

I told Darren about Louis Patch and his eyes flickered.

"Louis Patch, you say?"

I nodded. He glanced over his shoulder, and then in the other direction before leaning towards me. A tinge of something secret lingered in his voice. "We have to talk, man."

I was still holding the dinghy's rope to stop it drifting on the current. And Dad was walking from where he'd parked the Landcruiser. Whatever Darren wanted to say, I figured he didn't want heard by anyone else. He looked at my Dad who recognised him.

"G'day, Darren."

Darren nodded back. "Hey, Mr Mitchell."

Dad spotted Darren's empty wagon and rod. "Did you just arrive?"

A sly grin crossed Darren's face. "Nah, Mr Mitchell. I nicked 'em off some guy downriver." When Dad hesitated, Darren winked. "Just kidding. Yeah, I just got here and wondered how Robin caught this dinghy here. I should've guessed it was yours."

Dad nodded at Darren's cheeky humour. "Do you want to come out with us? We might end up catching something bigger."

Darren hesitated, looked me in the eye as he considered. I nodded to tell him it was cool. "Mr Mitchell, I'd like to talk to Robin about something."

Dad's active mind lit his quiet eyes as he watched Darren's hands. "It sounds like something big. This wouldn't relate to this morning, would it?"

Darren's bare toes dug in the dirt. "Not quite."

Dad glanced at me, then at the boat, and shrugged. "I can wait if you like."

Darren leaned closer to whisper. "Is your Dad cool with weird shit?"

What? "Weird shit?" I glanced at Dad who pretended to

be doing something with the dinghy. "He's open-minded, if that's what you mean."

"It's about last night. You might need to know."

My mind flashed back to the previous night. "Is it any crazier than having dreamt about it last night, only to learn today it was real?"

Darren's eyebrows lifted. "Did you...?"

I nodded, noting Darren didn't seem surprised. "I haven't told Dad, but we've talked about that kind of thing before. Is it like that?"

Darren passed me and headed for the dinghy. "Well, let's go. The fish won't catch themselves."

# CHAPTER 7

The Middleville summer sun is cruel, but its heat was worse than usual that morning. I was glad to have my hat that day, yet Darren didn't appear bothered by it. At least, the heat didn't bother him; something else did.

Dad took us upriver out towards the middle until we were between the Country Comfort Inn on the south bank and the opening for Grants Creek on the north. Flashbacks of the dream came to me. I looked at Dad, considered telling him to keep going instead of stopping, but stopped when I saw him gazing at Darren.

Darren was staring at Grants Creek too, his eyes open wide enough that his eyeballs could have rolled onto the dinghy's floor - or into the river. His fingers twitched. He tried to stop them by gripping his fishing rod tighter. That made his arms shake.

"Can we keep going further, Dad?"

Dad's eyes flicked to me, back to Darren, and he nodded as he steered the boat further along the river. All the while, we both watched Darren as he relaxed the further we progressed.

When we were far enough away that Darren calmed, Dad stopped the outboard motor.

"I guess this is as good a place to fish, boys."

Soon we had baited hooks and cast our lines.

"Tell me your story, Darren," I said.

My friend glanced back in the direction we'd come from, drew a breath, and began.

My brother Albert and me were out for a walk last night near Grants Creek. We didn't have any plans. Just getting out of the house while Dad was drinking. He can be a rough nut if he's had enough.

I'm not sure why, but Albert headed back home for

something he forgot. He'd forget his head if it wasn't screwed on, you know.

This must've been about half-past eight; I reckon an hour or two after sunset. So it was dark enough I could spook you with my eyes and teeth. Just kidding, mate, but you get the idea. It was still light enough, I could see by the streetlights they have over from the new bridge. And the moon.

I heard a fella swearing, knew it from somewhere, but couldn't tell who it was at first. It came from the creek's mouth, near where it flows into the river. I thought it was one of my brothers. So I had peeped from the bridge.

It was a white fella but. I could tell even in the dark, thanks to the moon overhead. Its light reflected off the river water, making him more shadowy but not so much I couldn't tell he was pale. Then I recognised his shape. It was Patchy.

I was about to call out to him, hey. That's when I saw her. She was standing above the creek bank, looking down at him from the grass. She looked sexy as anything. Too good looking, if you know what I mean. And I couldn't take my eyes off her.

She called out to him. "Louis," she said. Her voice was low, but the breeze carried her voice to me.

Patchy jumped. He mustn't have known she was there. When he turns around, she meandered down the bank like she was on an escalator at the Shopping Fair. Know what I mean? Too easy for her. I would step down, trying not to fall, but she either knew the ground well or she floated down. I reckon it was the floating. That was the second thing I noticed about her.

Louis stood back to watch as she came down to the creek and waded into the creek's water. Then she takes her clothes off. So far, they hadn't noticed me, so I'm happy enough to watch, but I sneaked through the grass to watch closer. I never seen white folks do it before.

Naked as the day she was born, this girl is dancing in the water. She lifts the water to herself and splashes it over her shoulders and hair.

Patch must have been turned on. I know I was. She looked great. Moonlight reflected from the wet parts of her skin so she looked like she glowed, only it looked more blue than silver. Her lips, they were shiny too, and her teeth stood out. I wished I was down there instead of Patchy. He walks closer to her, saying something I can't make out.

She danced away from him. He jumped closer, and she dodged. They were play-chasing. She laughed and giggled because he couldn't catch her. I knew she was playing him, even when he finally grabbed her. She let him, I reckon.

Then they held each other. I watched them kissing. I was about to get up and go because this was boring me to shit. Okay, that's a lie. I stayed like glue held my eyes to her.

But I wish I didn't.

They swayed together, back and forth, and they were kissing. Not just pecks on the face either. Their lips locked in full-on pashes that soon changed to bites and nips at lips, neck, and shoulders until I hear Louis cry out in pain.

"Bitch, that hurt!"

And she laughs.

"No, I mean it."

He tried to pull away, but she was strong and gripped hard, laughing and calling him a baby. Then she made singing noises, her voice like honey, or like those sirens in the Greek stories we had to read in eighth grade. Patch calms at the sound, resists her less, and soon they embrace again.

Soon they're moving towards the flat part of the riverbank. If you look there, you'll notice a log still. That's where they sat, and he removed his shorts and threw them into the grass. He was ready when she straddled him. And they were moving and stuff, moaning and groaning, you know what I'm talking about. But before they made the sounds I've heard come from me parents' room at night, a loud crack reaches my ears. Patchy jerks upward, screams, and his head falls over her shoulder. From where I watched, still hidden, I couldn't see his face, but his head jerked upward and back, I reckon he hurt bad. Then I saw the side of his face. His mouth hung open like those clowns at the sideshows, only he wasn't eating ping pong balls. Blood dribbled from his mouth and she was laughing and squeezing him harder. Crunches and crackles filled the air. They must have been his broken bones.

I reckon she crushed him with her squeezes.

When she finished, he dropped to the ground, limp, dead. For a second, she looks at him but then flicks her face towards me. I damn near shit myself. Had I gasped or cried aloud and she heard me? Maybe. And, mate. Her eyes! They shone an evil colour like radioactive blood.

I held my breath, still as a statue, wishing I had more long grass to hide me. But I couldn't move without attracting more attention, although I reckon she knew I was there.

We must have been twenty metres apart from each other. With the moon giving most of the light, I held my breath. Bugger me. The longer I stayed still, the more my foot itched. Then my leg. I didn't dare move. If she had only heard me, but not seen me, my scratching would have caught her attention. Dead set. The urge to scratch grew. I tensed the muscles there to distract myself. And still she watched in my direction. For how long, I don't know.

At last, she turned back to Patchy's limp body, and I shit you not. She lifted him with one hand and flung him at the thick tree that grows in the middle of Grants Creek. You know the one. It looks like it's dead because it has no leaves, but I tell you, that tree is strong. She threw him hard enough into the air that I heard the crack of his body hitting the trunk. He sounded soggy against it, like when you stab a fish to gut it, only louder. And a branch went through his back and out his chest. Patch's head flopped, his open eyes looking at me with his mouth open.

I couldn't wait longer. My legs were like jelly, but they did their duty in running me away. And she laughed. At me? I don't know. Maybe, or maybe she was laughing at Patchy in the tree. I didn't care. I kept running until I reached home, her laughter still filling my ears and head.

When Darren finished, Dad and I were silent. No words could do justice. But my father noticed something. My hands were shaking.

Years ago, Darren had told me a story about a ghost he knew and talked to at night. That was in third grade. Later that night, I woke up screaming from a nightmare that Darren was telling the ghost to kill me. A stupid dream and all. Dad had come rushing into my room because my scream curdled his blood, he said. He blamed me for reading scary stories before going to sleep. I didn't tell him it was Darren's tale. The next day, I approached Darren at school and told him his story was rubbish, not true, and he laughed. Of course, it wasn't true, he told me with a huge grin.

This time, I looked at Darren. My dream the night before matched his story. Darren told the truth this time. It wasn't a ghost story between mates to make one of us wet our bed in the middle of the night.

Dad's expression told me he believed it too.

Should I? I wondered.

Darren looked at me. "There's one other thing, Robbo. I forgot to mention it because I saw something else that night."

"What?"

Darren swallowed again, coaxed his reel a few times, and looked at Dad, then at me. "I saw you watching from the bridge."

Dad's voice reflected his shock. "Robin? I thought you were at home."

I looked at my father, saw the disbelief in his eyes, and realised he thought I was at the bridge. I shook my head.

"It wasn't his body, Mr Mitchell."

"What do you mean?"

"Robin was dream-walking. His body was safe in bed."

Darren's eyes watched me, full of knowing. Dad looked at Darren; if his jaw dropped lower, it would have landed in the bait bucket. Then he looked at me.

"What are you talking about?"

I swigged my cup of water. "Dad," I said. "I didn't tell you. I dreamt of Louis Patch last night and saw him meet a girl. But I didn't see him killed in the dream. I woke before that happened. You were watching a movie when I woke."

Dad's expression changed. A look of knowing shone in his eyes as he chewed his lip. "I see." His voice trailed.

"Dad?"

He looked up at me.

"I didn't kill him, Dad."

He gave a small snort and smiled. "I know you didn't." After a moment, he noticed Darren and I both watching him. "It's okay, boys. I'm not telling the police. Your secrets are safe."

"I'm not telling anyone what you said either, Darren."

# CHAPTER 8

Dad cut the fishing short after hearing Darren's story and my dream. The act of catching a fish, gutting and cleaning it for dinner didn't seem right. A friend of Dad's once told me how he worked in a chicken factory. After electrocuting the chicken, a conveyor belt carried it to where Dad's mate worked. He had to pluck them before the chickens were cleaned again. The smell of its death, the blood, and the bleach, put him off eating chicken ever again.

This is funny to say. That night, fish lost its appeal for us. Even if we had chips too. Thankfully, we had some juicy steaks to eat that night. Apart from agreeing what not to eat, we said nothing while I chopped up the salad and Dad cooked the steak, and chips baked in the oven. Steak burgers, salad and chips with tomato sauce. The dinner for kings.

We were about to dig into the food when the phone rang. Dad's rule was simple: don't answer the phone while eating dinner. Let the machine answer it. Once, I had asked him why he thought like that, and he replied: I have the phone for my convenience, not everyone else's. These days, with mobile phones, that means more than it did then.

The dutiful electronic servant played the greeting recorded by Dad and me. It beeped. Another voice played. I didn't recognise it at first: Norman's mother.

"Hello, Robin. I hoped you would make it this afternoon. I'm sorry to have missed you. Can you call back?"

Upon hearing Mrs Cole's voice, Dad nodded for me to answer the phone. I was too late reaching it, so I picked up the phone and tapped out Norman's phone number.

Ella picked it up on the first right. "Hello?"

A gooey sensation exploded in my stomach at her voice. Words clung to my mouth, not wanting to escape.

"Hello?"

"Ella!" Her name sprang from my mouth. "It's Robin. Is everything okay?"

Ella must have covered the mouthpiece. Muffled words reached my ear as she told Mrs Cole who was calling. The sounds of the phone moving, its cord whipping and hitting something else, then Norman's mother's voice shot me with disappointment.

"Robin? It's Mrs Cole. We didn't see you at the hospital." She sounded like I had fallen short of her high expectations for me as Norman's friend.

"Sorry I didn't make it. How is Norman?"

She huffed. "He's still sleeping. But his fingers twitched a few times today."

Hope filled me. "Is he waking up?"

"No. The doctors won't say much, but we are hoping." A pause. "You are coming in tomorrow, aren't you? I had hoped you would be a reliable friend for Norman in his time of need."

Anger stabbed from inside me. How dare the bitch? But she was an adult, so I still held some respect for her.

"Mrs Cole, I already apologised for not being there today. Something came up that-"

"Something like playing with your friends? Playing computer games, maybe?"

What? Any reply I wanted to make hid in the back of my throat.

From nowhere, Dad appeared at my side, took the phone from my hand and listened. Mrs Cole's voice still came to my ears as she told me how unhappy she was that I didn't turn up for Norman.

Dad's calm voice was like clouds masking lightning. "My son was busy with me today, Ruth."

I didn't catch her words, but Mrs Cole's surprise was clear.

"If you turn on the news, you will learn that Frank Patch's son died last night. Robin was helping the police with their enquiries."

Mrs Cole spoke again. Dad responded in an even and calm tone. "No, we don't know what happened to Louis. But Robin wasn't in a state to visit the hospital today. You can appreciate that."

Mrs Cole's voice again.

Dad turned his gaze towards me. "Robin, do you want to visit Norman tomorrow?"

I nodded.

"I will bring him tomorrow afternoon after work." He paused. "I'm sorry to hear what happened to Norman. He's a good kid." He nodded as Mrs Cole spoke on her side. "Okay, I'll let him know. Bye."

He returned the phone to its cradle and looked at me. "Mrs Cole apologised. Sometimes she doesn't realise she's not the centre of the universe. Many people are like that." He winked.

"She's worried about Norman."

"Yeah, she is." Something caught his attention. Maybe he remembered dinner because he nodded towards the dinner table. "Your steak's getting cold."

I was in Dad's fishing boat, floating on the murky water. Waves lapped at the boat, fast, rocking the vessel and me in it. The urge to vomit rose, bile burned my throat and mysterious music filled the air. I looked for the outboard motor and reached for it, only for the pull-cord to break in my hands and slip back inside. Angry, I punched at the motor and searched for the oars. But there were no oars. Only two large sticks of licorice sat there.

A splash caught my attention, and I peered through the darkness to see what it was.

There, on a rock in the middle of the river stood Louis Patch. A hole in his chest, large enough for my fist, allowed me to see the moonlight on the water behind him. He spotted me, nodded, and walked across the water towards the boat. I'm unsure what I expected, but it wasn't his smile. A genuine grin as the water splashed his ankles with each stride.

"Robin," he said. "Watch out for her, man. She's a man

eater."

Then before I could reply, my stomach lurched, and I flew through space. All the equipment from Dad's boat were in the air too, scattered like a cloud of confetti. Gravity was on holiday, and I floated there, turning in space until I faced the moonlit river ten feet below me.

Then the vision flooded my horror-struck eyes.

Sharp teeth. A large open mouth filled with pointy razor-sharp choppers. The unmistakable stench of fish guts filled my nose as the shark's jaws captured my head and jerked hard.

I woke with a scream. Dad's feet stomped on the wooden floorboards as he dashed towards my room. A light switch flicked. Light flooded my room. Blinded me.

He gasped.

Then I became conscious of the pain on my face. It hurt so bad, fiery hot like hot knives had streaked across my skin. Something dropped on my hand. Hot, then cold in the summer night's air. My gaze dropped, and in that instant, upon the sight, I fainted.

I woke to find myself in my bed. Pain seared through my skin still, but otherwise it was fine as long as I didn't move. Dad sat beside me, and another man stood nearby.

Dad's voice. "He's waking."

Dryness in my throat hurt me to swallow. My words didn't come.

"Don't talk," the man I now recognised as Doctor Trimble said. "Just relax, Robin."

Something constricted my head and face. My fingers reached for it. Bandages?

"Just nod or shake," the doctor said. "Do you know what happened?"

I shook my head. Then I remembered. "The dream." My voice sounded alien, like a corpse's, only not as nice.

Doctor Trimble gave my father a quizzical look. "A dream?"

"Water."

Dad hurried away to find a glass while the doctor leaned over me and examined my face. His careful fingers lifted the gauze from my face, surprise written on his face as though with a felt pen. The sound of the kitchen tap, followed by Dad's footsteps approaching. Doctor Trimble touched my face. Less pain this time.

"How does that feel?"

"Sore. But getting better."

Dad peered over the doctor's shoulder. "What the hell?"

Doctor Trimble turned to Dad. "I've seen nothing like it. Read about it in a book, but-" He looked back at me again and lifted more of the bandage. His jaw dropped open. "I don't believe it."

"What?" I still didn't know what they saw.

Dad and the doctor were both blinking and dumbstruck until I repeated my question. Then Dad picked up something from my desk - a Polaroid - and held it beside my face as though to compare. "Jesus Christ."

The doctor lifted what I recognised as my father's Polaroid camera, aimed at me, and blinded me with the flash.

"What is it?" I asked. "What's going on?"

"In a moment." The doctor shook the new photo, scrutinised it again next to my face, and gasped. "Unbelievable."

Sick of waiting, I snatched away the recently-shot picture to examine it. Red vertical lines covered my face as though I had scraped my fingers from my throat up my face to the scalp. At a guess there were about twenty-or-thirty of the scratches. Five-or-six of them originated from large round blotches, a deeper crimson than the lines.

With my thoughts scrambled like a Rubik cube, I paused so I could process everything.

Then I noticed my pillow near the foot of my bed. Deep and rich red splotches of blood covered its once pristine whiteness to resemble another Turin shroud. Images of the dream flashed by my mind's eye. The doctor turned the first photo for me. I fought the urge to vomit in shock.

The photo revealed my face, torn, ripped, and shredded at the surface by long bloody lines. Some lacerations were deep, etched into my flesh to reveal bits of bone in my cheeks. One was a hole in my cheek.

"Shit!" Not one to swear in front of my father, I couldn't hold back the word. "What the hell?"

Dad muttered. "It was even worse before I took the photo. I thought your head would fall off."

Doctor Trimble's voice trembled. "You really don't know what happened, Robin?"

I shook my head, still staring at my barely-recognisable face in the photo. "I had a dream."

"What happened in the dream?"

I summarised it, mentioned the shark jumping from the water and grabbing my head, how I remembered screaming. I also told them about seeing Louis walking across the water like he was Jesus Christ as a roguish teenager.

"Who is Louis Patch?"

My father took away the photos. "Someone from Robin's school died the other night. Robin's having nightmares about him."

The doctor examined my face again. "Self-mutilation during dreams is one thing. Even stigmata, which I've read about but not seen. But this..." He searched for a word. "This rapid healing. If I'd never seen it, I wouldn't believe it."

Through my window, I watched the first golden rays of sunshine rise and splash across the horizon across the tin roofs of the other houses. The night seemed like a bad dream itself.

"How long ago did it happen?"

"About five hours ago." Dad looked at the doctor. "What do we do? Will it happen again?"

Confident in my experience, my doctor's face was a picture of confusion and disbelief. He shrugged. "Your face is clear now. It's like it never happened."

Yet the photos told a different story.

# CHAPTER 9

"Are you sure you're well enough to visit Norman?"

I paused from drying my hair. "Yeah, I think so."

Despite the night's events, I was fine. Not even tired. I recalled the dream. If I hadn't seen the Polaroid shots of my facial gashes, the whole night could count as a bad nightmare. For me, it may as well have been pure fabrication.

After gelling my hair, I stepped from the bathroom and stopped in its doorway. Dad was standing in the hallway, looking at the wall. So far, he hadn't noticed me as he gazed at the photos of Mum, my little sister Anne-maree, and me. Mum and Anne-maree had died over ten years ago in a hit-and-run when I was five. A wet trail shone from his cheek as he lifted a hand towards Mum's picture, then my sister's, and mine.

At that moment, it occurred to me. He was so worried about me. Perhaps I should have taken my head out of my arse and considered him.

So far, Dad remained unaware of me standing there. Quiet as a mouse, I tiptoed back to the bathroom where I counted fifteen seconds to myself before coughing hard on my way out the door.

Dad turned towards me, sunglasses on his face, mirrored glasses that reflected my image. The tiniest remnant of the tear trail remained. Didn't he realise sunglasses only brought attention to them?

"Future's that bright you need sunglasses, eh?" I said, hoping he'd catch the song reference enough to laugh.

He managed a smile. "Yeah."

"Dad, what about you? You've been up all night looking after me." I pointed to the specks of grey in his hair. "I don't remember you being that grey yesterday."

He lifted a hand towards them, and I winked at him.

"What do you expect, Cisco?" he cracked, play-punching my shoulder.

"Aw, Pancho," I laughed a moment before turning serious. "Dad, are you sure you're right for it? You look tired as hell."

He snorted with a tight smile. "Nice. Next you'll say I'm getting old. Are you ready?"

"Yeah."

"Your hair looks like you stuck your finger in the power point. Look at those spikes!" I lifted an indifferent eyebrow when he pretended to mess my hair. "Do you often do yourself up for Norman, or are you hoping someone else is there?"

I could only snort in response. "You never know, Dad."

He sniffed, pulled a face, and waved the air near his nose. "I recognise my aftershave. Didn't even know you had more than bum fluff on your face, kid."

We arrived at Norman's room mid-afternoon. As usual, Mrs Cole was sitting there in the same chair as always, her back to the glass window which allowed a view of the trees outside.

"Robin." She nodded. "I'm glad you could make it."

"What happened to your hair?"

Maybe I had used too much gel.

"There's nothing wrong with his hair."

I turned towards the familiar voice and my heart stopped. Maerie stood in the doorway to the en-suite, something I never thought a comatose patient needed. A mysterious smile crossed her face as she appraised me, her eyes roaming from my head to toe. "It's one of the modern styles."

On the surface, it was a nice thing for her to say in my defence. But something lurked behind her shiny hazel eyes. The kind that reminded me of a cat eyeing its prey.

"Hi, Maerie."

"Robin."

She walked past me with a dancer's rhythm and grace. For the briefest time, I even thought of myself with her. But I shook away the feeling. She was Norman's girl, not mine, even if he never told me.

"Take a seat," she said, offering my father a chair. "You look like you've been up all night, Mr...."

"Mitchell," he said, with a nod. "Mr Mitchell."

Such an old-fashioned guy.

Maerie faced me in the manner of a church girl. The kind with a mouth in which butter never melts. "Did you bring your Walkman? I think Norman missed the music yesterday."

"Sure did." Walkman in hand, I approached Norman and whispered to him. "Hey, mate. I got you some more tunes." Lowering my voice to a whisper, I added, "Don't tell your Mum about the second one."

It was Samantha Fox's Touch Me. Norman had bought two posters of her six months previous. One showed Samantha wearing only skimpy underpants, a shirt slung over her shoulder; the other was a fully-clothed Fox reclining on a recording studio's equipment. He'd sneaked them home from Kmart and hung the tame version on the wall. The other one he stuck to the ceiling above his bed. Norman and I had laughed at that, making jokes about what he'd be doing later. His mother came in and saw them, but said nothing. However the next day, the semi-naked Sam Fox had disappeared while Norman was at school. When asked, Mrs Cole feigned ignorance, but Norman later found it crumpled in the bin. So the song on the Walkman was our in-joke.

If Norman heard what I said, I don't know. I half-expected Maerie to comment about the tape like she had the other day. But she didn't mention it.

Looking around for a chair, I noticed it was only the four of us with Norman. Maybe I wasn't casual enough with what I said. "Is Ella not here?"

"She's gone to the toilet," Mrs Cole said, her eyes focused on me. "Get a chair from outside."

But I spotted a plastic chair in the en-suite, the plastic garden type they have for patients to sit in while showering. Figuring Norman was getting sponge-bathed by some hot nurse (or maybe a butch one) I took it.

Dad and Mrs Cole were talking about my morning with the police and Louis Patch's murder, the news of which grabbed the bottom of The Daily Sentinel's front page. My name didn't make the paper as the "youth questioned by detectives", thankfully, but Dad figured Mrs Cole would know, anyway.

Maerie was sitting next to Norman, holding his hand. Outwardly, she focused on Norman, smoothing her fingers over his. But something in her expression told me she was listening to the whole thing.

She noticed me and turned her gaze to me. "I understand Louis Patch died."

Silence filled the room. An uncomfortable silence. Mrs Cole and Dad looked up in our direction. I shifted in my chair.

"Yes." Awkwardly, I glanced at my father whose features remained placid, masking his thoughts.

Maerie looked at my father, Mrs Cole, then back to me. "Why aren't you happy about it?"

Unpleasant silence again. Maerie's eyes bored into mine with a merciless intent. Did she enjoy this?

Dad cleared his throat, but I answered anyway.

"He bullied Norman a lot. I know that." I thought a moment. "But he's still a person. I remember when Louis and I were friends in first grade, before I met Norman. His parents and family are hurt through his death."

Maerie said nothing. Just gazed at me with a blank expression. Did she feel nothing? Yes, I felt good for Norman because Louis was the worst bully, the most violent one, and would no longer bother him.

Footsteps at the door distracted us.

In came Ella, looking beautiful. Tired, but beautiful, despite the red that rimmed her eyes. She smiled upon seeing me. "Robin! How are you?"

"Great," I answered, sitting taller, but not too tall, just in case.

"We were talking about Louis Patch," Maerie told her. "He's dead."

Ella looked surprised, but not by the news because she knew already. She glanced at me then back at Maerie. "Yeah. It was on the news last night." Grabbing her chair, she moved it away from Maerie and towards me.

The closeness, although not touching, was delicious, heady; it made me a little dizzy.

"Mum told me you were with the police yesterday."

"Yeah. Asking me questions about Louis."

Ella's forehead crinkled. The image her face presented remains with me nearly thirty years later. So beautiful. "I don't understand. Why are they asking you?"

"Someone told them about the run-in we had on Wednesday at the school."

Ella's surprise mirrored mine. "That's stupid. Did they talk to Randall?"

I shrugged. "No idea."

"You know Richard Crane's father is a detective?"

"He's the one who questioned me."

As I was about to mention my suspicions of Matthew Stubbs talking to Richard, who would have told his father about the school incident, the same crawling sensation in my head happened again. This time, it wasn't as bad as the other day. It was stealthier, like a thief in the night; light fingers rifling through my mind. Feather light, yet purposeful.

A light feeling filled my head, gave me the same dizzy feeling. I shook my head to clear it, then I saw Maerie's cold Bela Lugosi stare upon me. A shudder flooded through me, and my gaze dropped towards her throat. At that moment, a flash came to mind, and just as quickly, Ella's voice caught my attention.

She waved her hand in front of my eyes. "Robin. Are you okay?"

My eyes blinked as I willed away my embarrassment. Did she think I was perving at Maerie? Worse, did Maerie think I was doing it to her?

"Yeah. Must be the heat."

Ella stood. "Let's go for a walk," she said. "Help clear your head."

Surprised at the opportunity, I glanced towards Dad. His calm features betrayed nothing, apart from his eyes' slight squint. He gave a slight nod in my direction, and I knew.

"Yeah, sure," I replied and stood to follow her.

Maerie's face turned to follow me out the door, and it wasn't until we were halfway down the corridor that I realised the sensation faded.

Ella led me to the lifts where she pressed a button and we waited. "Are you still feeling off?"

I looked at Ella. "No, it's gone. Maybe the walk is working."

Ella's voice was low, like she didn't want anyone else to overhear. "More than that. I'll tell you more outside."

# CHAPTER 10

At the bottom level, Ella and I walked past the hospital's lobby into the bright sunshine outside. A large willow tree's wide canopy provided cool shade over the bench on which we sat.

Ella regarded me again with studious eyes. "Is the crawly feeling still in your head?"

"What? How did you know?"

Ella snorted. "It happened to me too. Twice; once on Wednesday, and again yesterday." After a glance to ensure no one was present, she lowered her voice to a half-whisper. "Have you noticed? There's something about Maerie."

She laughed when I hesitated to answer, which caused me to smile. "She's eccentric." I nodded. "And she stands up to your mother too."

Ella's laugh sounded good, the kind to make my ears melt with sighs. "Yeah, she does that." More giggles escaped, then her tone turned serious. "What do you find weird about her?"

"Strange? As in the way she stares at me?"

Ella levelled her eyes. "It's not about you, Robin. But yes, her stares, her words, her way of speaking, and the way things happen when she's nearby."

I raised my fingers to score what I'd noted, mentioning them as I did: the headaches and nose bleeds, the way she talks, the way she knows what songs are on the tape I played for Norman. Ella nodded for each thing I noted until I stopped at the song. "Could you gather the song from the headphones?"

She shook her head. "No. But what about the machine in the room, the EEG?"

"Absolutely!" Who could overlook the way it spat paper?

"It happened again today when she arrived, before you

and your Dad came. I mentioned the paper spits yesterday to the doctors who set up another machine. The replacement does the same."

I took a breath to consider. Somehow this was not what I had in mind when I came outside with Ella. But we were talking easier than in the hospital room.

"Doesn't it measure brain wave activity?"

Ella nodded with a sage-like expression. "Yeah, but it doesn't mean he's waking. There are no other signs of that."

Ella fell silent, her candid eyes unfocused while they stared into space as she drifted. I remained quiet, believing it was best for her. Part of me wanted to place my hand on hers or even an arm round her, but I stopped. There was still the question of John O'Sullivan. Her comment on Wednesday showed she had second thoughts about being with him because of the likes of Matthew Stubbs' friendship with him. But it would be okay to place my arm round her in comfort as Norman's friend. Right?

Then she blinked and the moment vanished.

"There's also the way Mum changes when she Maerie visits," Ella said, wiping her eye with a finger. "You didn't see it yesterday. Maerie held a complete conversation with her. Mum just nodded and took it all in."

"Maybe she's happy that Norman has a girlfriend, and she doesn't want to upset him in case he can hear everything."

Disbelief mixed with sarcasm filled Ella's expression. "You are kidding, right?"

"I know your mother is - what's the word? - dominating and my-way-or-the-highway, but she's not all bad."

Ella shook her head a moment, a patient smile on her face. "Get real. Mum's a bloody cow with that stuff. She gets an idea in her head and you've more chance of a pit-bull terrier letting go of your hand than her changing her mind."

I fought to hold back the laughter, but failed. "Yeah, okay, you're right. I just didn't want to insult your mother. But I saw her have words with Maerie on Wednesday. So I don't get what you mean."

"You saw her in the normal phase," Ella said. "Listen, yesterday, Maerie comes in, wearing the same dress you saw on her the other day. Mum gave her the icy response, the old you're-not-good-enough-for-my-boy look. Then she sees Maerie has a bunch of flowers, orange roses, which are Mum's favourite. Maerie gives them to her. At first, Mum is reserved. Polite. But she's not giving in to an obvious ploy. Maerie suggests that Mum smells the roses, which she does. Next, Mum is almost dry-humping Maerie like she were the best thing in the world."

On its own, I had to agree with Ella; it was strange for Mrs Cole. But Ella hadn't finished.

"Mum was so rapt in talking with Maerie, she forgot it was time to go home. I had to remind her three times. It wasn't until Maerie left that Mum realised." Ella paused a moment to let everything sink in for me.

"So she enjoyed talking with Maerie? Is that it?"

"When Maerie walked out the door, Mum shook her head as though waking from a dream. And she hated Maerie again."

For all the time I've known Norman and Ella's mother, I've never thought her two-faced. Ella seemed surprised by it, too, and I wondered what Mrs Cole said about me when I was absent. But then, she always spoke forthrightly with me. A terrible idea crossed my mind.

"Ella," I asked. "Have I done that with Maerie?"

She shook her head. "No. I questioned myself too."

"I don't believe so." Ella appeared relieved at the news. "Besides, you were with it enough to take me outside to talk."

Now was the time to ask. "What about John? Has he noticed anything?"

Ella's expression darkened a little, her lips paling a shade. "No. And I don't want him here."

I lifted an eyebrow to question.

"John and I haven't been together for about a week or two now."

It's selfish, I know. I couldn't help but think God exists upon hearing her say it. I held back my joy at her words.

"Which brings me to the next question," she said.

"What's that?"

"How do you feel about skating tonight?"

If not for the bench, I'd have fallen in shock. "Skating?" I hemmed. "Yeah, sure." At least it wasn't the Mexican Stand bar, but it wouldn't have mattered. My shock was at Ella beating me to the punch. I wanted to ask her out, not the other way round. "But one thing..."

Ella looked straight in my eye. Was that slight curl at her lip's corner a hidden smile? "What?"

"If all goes well, would you like to go to the water-slide?"

"We'll see." She stood, took two steps towards the hospital building, and looked over her shoulder. Yep. She was smiling. "But no Norman talk, okay?"

Like the Ferris Bueller song said: oh, yeah.

# CHAPTER 11

"A date?" Dad's voice showed as much excitement as I felt. He took one hand from the steering wheel to ruffle my hair and laughed. "My son, the Romeo." He glanced back at the road and back to me again. "So was it the aftershave or your sick act?"

Somehow, Dad thought my wooziness at the hospital round Maerie was just a ploy.

"A gentleman never kisses and tells," I answered in a mysterious voice.

Dad snorted. "A gentleman? Ha! You're my son; you can't fool me." He braked the car at the red traffic lights and grinned at me again. Then he read something in my expression. "What's wrong? Didn't you want the date?"

I grinned back. "Hell, yeah." I didn't tell him Ella asked me, though, since he might have teased me about that, too. "But the sick thing wasn't an act."

Concern crossed his face. "But you're feeling all right now, yeah?"

I nodded. "I was off-colour at the hospital on Wednesday and blamed the hot day."

"But it was Ella's hot looks, right?" Dad couldn't resist the laugh when he could find it.

"Yeah, she's hot, but it was Maerie."

Dad's face remained impassive as he glanced at the traffic light again and back to me. "Maerie? You have a thing for her too?"

"No."

"She's got a thing for you?"

"Dad!" I mock-protested. "No." He laughed at my exasperation, but the traffic light changed and he had to drive again. I told him about Wednesday; the headaches, Maerie's possible connection, and the weird feelings inside my skull.

My father listened, nodded occasionally, and said nothing more until I told him it had happened that day too.

"And you think Maerie did that?"

I nodded.

At the time when I thought Dad would remark, he didn't. Instead, he kept driving for about a block before I thought to talk again.

"Ella said she noticed something odd, too, with her mother."

At those words, Dad laughed. "She's always been unusual, that woman. Years ago, she used to try controlling everyone -- even me -- at school."

"No, a different weird. I saw part of it too. You know how she acts like she doesn't respect anyone?"

Dad nodded.

"You should have seen her butt heads with Maerie when they first met. At first, she was nobody's good enough for her boy. Maerie stood her ground and answered back. Today, Mrs Cole is almost humping her like a dog."

Dad remained quiet and only nodded. Wheels and cogs turned behind his eyes, and his face turned serious. He was silent until we arrived home and stopped the Landcruiser.

"I'm happy you have a date with Ella tonight," he said. "She's a nice girl, but a thought occurred to me. You've been having nightmares, and last night, your face looked like an abattoir. I could yet turn vegetarian again. This morning it's clear as the day your were born. I can't help thinking it links with Norman."

Disappointment tinged my mood. I opened my mouth, and Dad lifted a finger to finish. "Don't you see what I'm saying?"

Was Dad telling me not to go out with Ella? I tried joking it off. "You know you sound like Mrs Cole, don't you?"

But Dad didn't take the bait. "Doesn't it seem strange to you? Should I show you the photos?"

The image of my ripped face hammered me into silence.

Dad nodded as I considered his words, watching my eyes. "Maybe you need time away."

"Maybe I need to enjoy myself and tonight's the right thing."

Dad's head jerked back in shock at my outburst. I surprised myself too. We stared off each other for a few seconds, like two wolves ready to fight, neither daring to flinch or show weakness. Then Dad sighed, opened his drivers door and stepped out. "Okay, kid, do what you want." He shut the door, said he'd give me space, and stomped up the house's front stairs.

I waited in the Landcruiser a few minutes to think about Dad's words. Probably what he wanted me to do. My thoughts returned to seeing him in the hallway earlier and how he looked at the family pictures. He was only worried for me. But I couldn't understand why he wanted me home instead of out skating with Ella.

Confused, I wandered through the house and found him on the back verandah with a can of Fosters in one hand. The phone was in his other hand. His expression lighter than it had been a moment ago, he lifted his head.

"What is it, champ?"

"I'm sorry, Dad." The words didn't come easy. I took a breath and continued. "But I'm still going out with Ella tonight. I've wanted to do this for a long time."

He sipped his drink and nodded. "Me too, Robin." He glanced at the phone. "Feel like pizza before you go?"

I looked at my watch. "Nah, I'd better change. Pizza Hut isn't far from the rink, anyway."

"Suit yourself."

I turned to go.

"Robin, there's one thing."

"What?"

"I meant what I said about Norman. Something's not right." He turned back to gaze at the mango trees in the yard, their blossoms and burgeoning fruit. "Now, hurry and go. I'm expecting company."

"Company?"

He grinned, slurped another sip, and belched. "Yeah, and a gentleman never kisses and tells."

"So you've kissed her, huh?"

We both laughed at that. I had hoped Dad would tell me more, but he kept his mouth shut tighter than a fish's arsehole. And that's watertight.

# CHAPTER 12

After another quick shower, which prompted more comments from Dad, I hurriedly dressed and made my way around to Ella's place in the next street. I needn't have worried. She was still showering when I arrived.

This time, her father met me at the door. I liked Mr Cole and often had more time for him. He was a lanky man whose eyes always sparkled above his moustache, which always reminded me of the pilots from World War II. The British flyers. Norman had told me his father had once been a Commando with the British before he met the woman who later became Mrs Cole. But he took to working in the Capricorn Bank since then.

"Rob!" His light British accent filled the air as he offered his hand. "How are you, lad?"

"Good, Mr Cole," I answered, holding back a grimace as his fist-of-iron grip squeezed me.

His eyes crinkled at the edges as he surveyed my appearance. "Ella's still in the shower. Come on in."

That afternoon, everything felt different when I entered. The house was a little darker than I remembered, or maybe I imagined it because of the nervousness in me.

"How do you reckon we'll go in the cricket?" Mr Cole asked as he beckoned towards the lounge chairs in the even darker living room.

"I'm hoping well," I admitted. "But I'm unsure. Mike Gatting is good as a captain."

He smiled with an approving nod. "Good answer. I believe it will be a 2-1 win in the Ashes."

Mr Cole (or Mike as he sometimes insisted I called him) was more relatable than Mrs Cole. At least, that's what I found. I always thought him cheerful, and now with his son comatose in a hospital, his mood betrayed little of his worry.

It was the classic "stiffer upper lip" routine I read about in the Biggles books when I was younger. And as chipper as I saw him, Norman assured me his father could be a hard taskmaster on him and Ella. That was usually about their performance in school because he valued education and its potential rewards.

He and I swapped back and forth with our conversation -- books, the cricket, and a few other little things -- until the taps squeaked in the shower and the sounds of water rushing stopped.

"She's still putting on her face," Mr Cole said. "Would you like a drink?"

I nodded my thanks. "Just water, please."

A moment later, he returned and handed me a glass of water so cold it already formed condensation on the outside.

Mr Cole plonked himself in his favourite chair and looked at me a second. "Thank you for being Norman's friend." His deep voice belied his lanky form. "I appreciate all you have been for him."

His words carried a final tone, almost pessimistic. Not his usual mood. Did he expect the worst for Norman?

"I'll always be Norman's friend. Even when we're old men."

Then he smiled, sunbeams from behind the clouds I failed to notice earlier. "Of course, you will. Tell me something. I understand he has a girlfriend who visits him in hospital, too. Marie?"

"Maerie."

"Yes. Maerie." He said the name again as though training his memory. "Have you met her before?"

I shook my head. "Only at the hospital, which is weird because I never knew about her."

"That's what I thought too." Then he leaned closer, lowering his voice. "I've been up there, too, and seen her. Something odd about her I can't fathom."

"Oh?"

"I've seen many things in my time when I visited India.

Not the Indian Rope Trick, but I've seen men float better than Doug Henning, and have even heard a snake speak almost like a human. But this girl is something peculiar. Yesterday, when I-"

"What are you two whispering about like old women?"

My interest was piqued so high, I almost didn't hear Ella come into the room.

Mr Cole never missed a beat as he looked up at his daughter. "Ah! Here she is. I wondered if you fell down the plughole."

He stood and took a step to the side as he looked at her. So did I. She was such a vision, it was hard to act nonchalant.

Ella looked at me, the hint of a sparkle in her eyes and smile. "Let's go."

"Do you kids want a lift?"

"No, thanks." Ella led the way out the door.

"Good to know you have legs that work," her father quipped. Before I could go, he whispered in my ear. "That girl Maerie. She has no shadow."

My head turned in shock. "What?"

"Are you going to let Robin go or do you want to take him out?"

He nodded at me as he realised my surprise. "Go on. Don't keep the lady waiting."

# CHAPTER 13

The dying day's sun drummed us with the last of its rays as we walked along Teal Street towards the hamburger joint near Kmart.

The meal's conversation revolved around a few things: Ella's repeating Year 11, decided by her mother although her grades were already satisfactory; her break-up with John O'Sullivan, related in part to Mrs Cole, but I suspected something else; and her dreams of becoming a journalist. By the time she finished telling me about journalism, a smile crossed her face as she told me, "Perhaps you should be a journalist. You kept me talking the whole time."

All I could do was hide a smile with another bite of my burger. Dad had insisted months earlier that I read Dale Carnegie's How To Win Friends and Influence People. People love talking about themselves; keep asking questions. Maybe Dad didn't think I'd use it to pick up girls, like Ella, but I liked how it worked.

"Talking to you is so easy," she commented. "It's like you relax me."

"I enjoy talking to you, too," I admitted.

"Or listening."

I laughed. "It's okay."

"What I don't understand is, why we didn't talk more before."

"One mystery of life, I guess." My eyes caught the sight of the sun's dying light. Clouds - a mix of red, orange, and pink - hung in the sky and waited for the night to swallow them. And I had an idea. "Are you ready to walk off the pizza?"

"Is this your attempt to watch the sunset with me?"

The thought had crossed my mind. "Would you like to watch it?"

"Answering a question with a question, huh?" A smile

slipped across her face. "I didn't come down in the last shower, you know."

"So you didn't fall from Heaven?" I asked and kicked myself for being such a drongo.

"Quit while you're behind." Ella winked as she stood. "Come on."

I wiped my mouth with a napkin, picked up my backpack and scooted past a few diners waiting in line. A shade of recognition made me turn round to see a familiar face: John O'Sullivan, Ella's ex-boyfriend. He was already at the counter and ordering his meal. I figured it best I turn and hurry out the door. Ella was already out the door, but I had to wait for a family of large people to squeeze through the door.

They were harsh-voiced, their words blasting, loud enough to -

I glanced. Why did I do it? I should have left without looking at him.

John was watching the incoming family, his attention attracted by their bellowing words. "I want the Whopper." "Why? One Whopper's not enough." Then he glanced back at me. Our eyes locked.

At first, it was fine. He nodded at me in greeting. Then his shrewd eyes flicked towards the door. I glanced, saw Ella in John's line of vision, and his expression changed. Surprise opened his eyes and realisation coloured his face, turned it to mute anger.

Too busy fuming at me, he ignored the attendant who had returned to say something to him. Then the father of the family bulldozed his way between us and blocked our lines of sight. The opportunity was too good to miss. I vamoosed out the door. Ella hadn't seen John. At least, she didn't mention him as we walked.

The Middleville Skating Centre was already open when we arrived. The heavy tones of John Farnham's You're The Voice rocked from inside and filled us as we entered and pushed our way past other teenagers either rolling their way onto the rink. Some beginners nearby tottered like drunk dancers before they fell unceremoniously to the ground. I already had my own skates in the backpack but still had to pay admission along with Ella.

Before long, we were gliding along the rink's perimeter. I loved skating, still do, but that night started well for me. Maybe it was the thrill of a Clayton's date, the kind you have when you're not calling it a date yet. The spinning lights above circled the rink with us, spraying circles of red, green, yellow and blue on the surface. Banarama's Venus rocked the night as we sped past slow skaters, avoiding the novices.

We must have been skating for about half an hour, I guess. It may as well have been five minutes for the fun I had with Ella. Laughing, wise-cracking at things, and then Prince's voice filled the arena with his song Kiss.

We drifted closer, slower, but still synchronised with each other. I figured we were close enough. My hand reached for hers which appeared stretched ready for that electrical first touch.

Nothing else mattered. The music faded away in my mind. It was just the two of us, the light touch of our fingers.

As though from the distance, I heard someone shout. Was that my name? I glanced too late.

Something massive bowled into me. Pain lanced through my arm. My feet flew into the air, level with my puzzled eyes as I crashed to the ground.

The impact forced the wind from me with a tortured grunt. Something like needles flared through right arm. Ella screamed, but I barely noticed it as I stared down the oncoming skater speeding straight for my face.

# CHAPTER 14

It was too late. I couldn't move out of the way. Too many people. The skater loomed large in my vision. My left arm covered my face.

Impact delayed.

The skater rose in the air, clearing me without touching, and his wheels clacked on the bitumen followed by a scrape as he spun and braked.

"Shit, mate," he said and offered me a helping hand. "Are you okay?"

Still stunned, I nodded. My right arm was sore but otherwise numb from when I landed on it. No broken bones. Just bruises. "Lucky you jumped."

"Lucky I bloody saw you." He had the sound of a farmhand from Marlborough with the cattle farms. Or even Barcaldine. "I nearly hit you."

"No harm done," I muttered.

He nodded, glanced at Ella with a grin, and was off round the rink again.

"What happened?" Ella asked, brushing something from the leg of my jeans.

"Somebody knocked me down. You saw nothing?"

She shook her head and looked across the rink. "No. But I was looking over there, near the canteen. Next thing I know, you're on the ground."

My eyes searched for any likely culprit but saw nothing. "Let's go."

We started again, gliding along the floor. Just as we reached momentum, a voice spoke from behind.

I turned in time to receive a knuckle sandwich and dropped to the ground. Another fist came at me. I blocked and saw Jason Baker's scowl. Ella screamed. I moved between her and Jason who advanced closer.

Soon Paul Thornton joined him. The two of them were friends of Louis Patch. My mind picked an odd time to do mathematics; two and two meant John O'Sullivan must be somewhere close.

I fended another blow away, this time from Paul.

"What the hell are you doing?" I kept rolling backwards, keeping in front of Ella to protect her from anything.

"You know why." Paul's shout filled the air. He glanced at Ella, looked at Jason who leered back at me, and turned back to me. "Johnno's off the scene two minutes and you're banging into his girl."

Ah! So that's what it's about.

Ella shouted. "John and I split up. Leave us alone."

But Paul ignored Ella's words. He jerked his head, cracking his neck, and moved towards me. But this time, I pushed at his shoulders, aiming the force up and back.

Surprised, his feet flew into the air as he tumbled to the ground. Karma's a rabid bitch.

Jason lunged for me. He wasn't wearing skates and had better traction.

A whistle blew somewhere. The song played by the DJ stopped, and the rink was silent save for two screams from different directions. Nearby, a few kids cried; their parents told us to take it elsewhere. Fists flew. Some landed on me. At least one landed in Jason's face. Paul was up and trying to stomp on my hands and legs with his skates.

Then a girl's scream filled the air. And Jason stopped punching and kicking at me. A crashing sound to my left punctuated the scuffle. Paul stopped punching me for long enough for us to glance and face someone else I couldn't see through my half-closed eyes and red pain. I could only make out a girl's shape. She lifted him by the ear, forcing a cry from him, and punched hard into his stomach. He groaned, dropped to the ground, and lay there like a ton of bricks.

I gingerly lifted myself from the ground. Hands helped me from behind, and I realised it was Ella.

So who decked Jason?

I turned to behold a familiar auburn-haired beauty.

"Maerie?"

Her mouth flickered in a brief smile before her eyes burned at our two attackers. Jason was holding his stomach and rolling on the ground in a moaning mess. Meanwhile, people milled round Paul whose moans and groans were barely audible from that distance.

Then I noticed a man, large enough to strain his security guard uniform's buttons, amble towards his. His porn-movie-star's moustache twitched under his bulbous nose as he approached.

"Look out," someone mumbled from nearby. "It's LA Law coming." And the crowd of gawkers dispersed from us.

The guard's eyes fixed on me as he pointed an authoritative finger at me. "You! Stay there." A smell of something rancid drifted across my nostrils when he was close enough to talk. Someone needed a shower. "What's going on here?"

"These guys attacked me."

"They're not the ones beaten to a pulp," he commented, taking in the scene.

Jason stood, glared at me. "I accidentally bumped into him, sir. He and this girl started punching into us."

Such a liar. Convincing too.

Maerie took none of it. "You and your boyfriend both barrelled into Robin. Then you started punching and kicking him."

Her voice's conviction froze Jason and the guard both. The guard's jaw hung slack. If he had been smoking, the cigarette would have dropped. He turned to Jason. "Is this true?"

Jason shook his head. "She joined in, too, and -"

"Are you saying a girl beat you up?" Ella cut in.

Jason's Adam's apple bobbed like a fishing buoy. "Y... No, I mean-"

The security guard regarded Jason's bleeding nose and mouth then watched another staff member haul Paul

Thornton towards us.

"You," he said, pointing at Paul. "What happened to you?"

Paul looked at me then at Maerie and nodded at her. "She pushed me over there."

A man sick of dealing with hormonal teenagers, the security guard sighed. Perhaps he wanted to pinch his nose to halt a migraine. He looked like it. To Maerie, he said, "Did you punch up these boys?"

Maerie showed no hesitation in her answer. "Of course. They deserved it and more."

"See!" Jason's voice cracked in amazement at Maerie's admission. "She's a crazy bitch!"

The guard held up a hand to silence Jason. "I've heard enough from you all. Come to the office. I'm calling the police to take you away to your parents. You can explain things to them."

Jason and Paul looked at each other, hiding a smirk between them. I remember the sinking feeling that washed over me because I didn't want another trip to the police station. Once was enough. We all started towards the office. Except Maerie. She stood her ground and stayed behind.

The guard noticed, reached out to place a hand between her shoulder blades to guide her, and she grabbed his hand. He hissed in pain and grimaced. "Let go of me."

Maerie pushed his hand away. "I'm not going with you."

Surprise filled his face. "What?"

"Take those boys." She looked at me. "Except for Robin. And Ella stays too. But take them."

"Listen here," the guard replied, "you're all coming with me."

Maerie's voice filled the rink. "Never. Touch me again, and you will suffer the consequences."

"Consequences?" The guard snorted in amusement and shook his head with a smile. "The only consequences are for you." He stepped forward and took her wrist.

Quick as a whip, Maerie reversed the hold and gripped his

wrist. Incredible strength blazed like lasers from her narrowed eyes into his.

Her voice was low, but the words were clear. "Go, fuck yourself."

Jason and Paul made an "oohhh" sound, the kind one makes when someone has crossed a line and is in big trouble. Even I was shocked.

The guard didn't even react, at least not how I expected. His eyes opened wide, large as Garfield the cat's eyes on three coffees, and his facial muscles tightened. He seemed to fight an internal battle and the tiniest whimper escaped despite his closed lips.

I glanced at Ella, Paul and Jason. They seemed equally mystified as the four of us watched the guard. Even his muscles seemed tightened, stiff as a corpse. One foot started to move, but then he seemed to change his mind. Sweat formed at his brow, beaded drops on his greasy skin. Then his shoulders relaxed, he shook his head, excused himself and left us.

By the time he reached the wooden barrier at the rink's edge, he attracted the curious gaze of everyone else. A staff member said something to him, which he ignored as he marched away towards the toilet.

Still surprised, I looked for Maerie but she was gone.

Jason whispered something to Paul and they quit the scene, heading in a beeline towards the exit. A similar urge passed over me as people re-entered the rink and the DJ spun another record, "When The Going Gets Tough". I always thought the lyrics were "go and get stuffed".

I nudged Ella who was still looking after the guard who had since disappeared into the crowd. "I think we'd better go."

"Are we supposed to follow him?" Ella asked. "He said he was calling the cops for us."

"I think he changed his mind."

"Then why don't we keep skating? Paul and Jason have pissed off."

As we started rolling around the rink's perimeter, shouting emanated from near the toilets. I didn't catch the words at first. Then we heard words we couldn't miss.

"Call an ambulance! The guard's stuck a toilet brush up his arse!"

# CHAPTER 15

People thronged towards the toilet to glimpse the guard with a toilet brush wedged in his anus. But we had different ideas. We figured it was best to go before people asked questions.

Outside, the warm night air still felt cooler than inside. Even with passing traffic, it was quieter, calmer. But it was Middleville.

Ella cast a longing look back inside the arena. "What a shame. I was enjoying tonight."

I laughed. "Yeah, me too."

"What are we going to do now?"

There wasn't much else to do in North Middleville on a Friday night, and we were too young to attend Flamingos night club.

"How about we go to Pondarosa?"

Ella looked at me like I suggested she eat cold liver. "Pondarosa? That's where all the sluts and boneheads hang out."

I'd been there at night a few times myself. Yeah, some colourful people went there, but they weren't all that bad. Still, Ella was allowed her opinion. "I don't have enough for taxi fare, anyway," I said, letting the idea slide.

"Shame the cinema is on the other side of town too."

I checked my digital watch's time. It was 8pm. No decent teenager would want to go home - on holidays.

"Want to watch a Friday night movie instead?"

"At my place?" Ella scrunched her nose. "Boring!"

"Okay," I laughed. "How about my place?"

The words slipped from my lips before I dwelled on what she might think. We had just played the "your place or mine" conversation without realising it.

"I bet you ask all the girls that."

"So far, yes."

Ella's eyes opened wide. "How many?"

"Just the one."

"I don't believe you." She laughed when I opened my mouth to protest. "It's okay. I know it's the truth. Norman would have told me if you had a girlfriend before."

"Do you often talk to him about me?"

Lost for words, she stopped to think. "He talks, I mean talked, about you often."

I snorted. "Yeah, Norman and his mouth, huh?" Then I went silent. Norman had kept his mouth shut about Maerie.

"Would you have kept a secret like that from him?"

I shook my head. Until then, I had thought Norman told me everything, so I told him my life too.

We headed around the corner, in the same general direction as home. A car drove by, its passenger wolf-whistling as it passed. "Thank you," I said after them, and Ella laughed.

"What do you think happened to the security guard?"

I allowed a smile. "He snapped. Probably having a mental breakdown, the poor guy."

"But isn't it funny how it happened after Maerie said that to him?"

"I thought you didn't want to talk about Maerie tonight," I reminded her.

"Hard not to when she turns up at the skating rink on the same night we're there," Ella replied. "And look at what happened."

That was a coincidence I couldn't shake. "Yeah, you have a point."

"She's like some kind of vampire," Ella stated aloud, which in the darkened state of Sherwood Street, the nearest streetlights being behind us or the traffic lights quarter of a kilometre away at Central Highway, is a creepy experience.

"A vampire?" I scoffed to talk myself out of the idea, which my mind entertained far too much. "They don't come out in the day, do they?"

"Why not? We still come out at night, don't we?"

"That's not the same. We don't shrivel up and die in the dark. Next you'll say they can glitter like those sparkly troll toys. Why do you think that?"

"Haven't you read Dracula?" she asked.

My jaw dropped. "You read Dracula?"

"Why so surprised? I am an educated girl." She playfully punched me before her voice returned to its serious tone. "Dracula could hypnotise his victims. He had that mental link with Mina Harker so he knew what Van Helsing and the others planned after he made her suck his blood."

"Gruesome girl." I grinned at her in the dark.

"I'm serious, Robin. Maerie seems to know things. I'd stake my life on it."

"Stake and vampires," I crooned. "Oh, my. You're beginning to sound like Norman and his D&D stuff."

"Maybe I'm closer to it than you think. John is still into D&D too."

I don't know what surprised me most: Ella mentioning John or his association with D&D. Neither one impressed me.

"Did you know John was at Rollo Burgers when we left?"

Ella shrugged. "So what?"

Shut up, Robin, I told myself. Shut up. Jealousy is not cool.

"I wonder if he was at the rink too," I added. "You know. David and Jason were there. He wasn't far away."

"Neither's Christmas, but Santa's not here, is he?"

"I wondered if he had set up the fight." My argument sounded weak the moment I voiced it.

Ella scoffed. "John doesn't hang with them much. At least not with Jason and David. He told me something about them that he didn't like."

"What?"

"It doesn't matter," she said. "Anyway, back to Maerie. You mentioned how you felt like she was in your head, right? I noticed what she did to my mother, and I know I felt something too. Do you think she can read our minds... like Dracula?"

"Even if she does," I answered. "That doesn't make her a vampire. Although I could almost see her dressed like Elvira. Do you remember the dress she wore when she first visited?"

"Got a thing for my brother's girlfriend, do you?"

Bingo. Ella's tone carried jealousy, just a hint. I smiled to myself, but I didn't want her to harbour it long. So I turned to look at Ella, her face illuminated now by the traffic streetlights at the corner of the Central Highway and Teal Street. The way her eyes reflected the lights and the thin film of perspiration glowed was awesome.

"I'm with you," I said. "Not her."

My hand reached for fingers which responded to my touch, holding mine as I held hers.

"Can we stop talking about Maerie?"

"As you wish," I answered. "Tell me more about what you're into."

The traffic lights bipped and ticked away to signal we could walk. We started across. "In a moment," she replied and remained quiet until we reached the other side.

It felt good to hold her hand, a memory I still hold today. One of the best from those days.

Upon crossing the street, we walked up the footpath's slight grade until we were under the branches of a tree overhanging from inside the corner house's yard. And she stopped.

"You know what?"

"What's that?"

"Do you remember the fight tonight when Jason and Paul were coming at us?"

Who could forget that? I nodded.

"You stepping in to protect me turned me on."

Did the shadows hide my blush? They didn't hide how her teeth shone from her smile, reflected by the dim light.

Her slender hand reached around my neck, gently pulled me down to her height, and her lips locked with mine. I'd kissed a girl once before. It was part of a dare in eighth grade. Long story short, that was my first kiss. They say you never forget them. Maybe that's true. But my second kiss was with Ella that night, and I remember that with greater clarity and more fondness.

Her lips were soft, caressed mine as though they were fingers. I recall the touch of her tongue, too, as it grazed mine. At first, it was tentative, and I reciprocated in kind. Then they danced. Not the shoving it into each other's throats (like the first). Then our lips parted, just enough to gain breath, yet we stayed mere centimetres apart, gazing in each other's eyes, our breathing slightly quicker.

Her voice came in a light whisper that aroused me in the semi-darkness. "You know something else?"

"What?"

"My mother's going to eat you for breakfast. I'm past her curfew."

I pressed my watch's light button and squinted. 8:45pm. "You're kidding."

I wanted to ask if John O'Sullivan used to bring her home on time, but I thought better of it.

She shook her head. "I'm not kidding. You know my mother well enough by now."

"Then you know I don't care. She hates me, anyway."

Ella shook her head. "No, she thinks the sun shines out your bum because you protected her little boy in school. She'd want you to marry him if it wasn't illegal."

I blanched. "Me and your brother? What kind of sicko is she?"

We laughed, holding hands as we walked to her place at Madding Street. And there, beside the bottle brush tree on the footpath outside her place, we gazed at each other again.

"Are you sure you don't want to come to my place?

Ella looked back at her house. The lights were off, but we saw the jumping flicker of the TV reflect through the windows. Either or both her parents were awake. Probably watching the Friday night movie on RTQ-7.

"Come on," I urged. "Be original. Say yes."

She bit her lip, considering it as she looked at her house and back at me. "What are you doing tomorrow?"

"Working at the water slide."

"You work there? I didn't know." She paused, a suspicious eyebrow raised as a smile blossomed from her lips. "Is that why you invited me on a date there?"

After being with her, I'd forgotten that. I smiled. "I'm working in the afternoon. But we could meet at night. Try the blue tube at night. It's unreal."

"I'll meet you there."

She stood on tiptoes and gave me another kiss. I held on and kissed more, enjoying her taste.

I'd have kissed again, but the front lights turned on and bathed us in a bright halo.

"Ella? Is that J-. Oh, it's Robin." Mrs Cole sounded almost disappointed. "Robin, it's time for Ella to come inside now. It's late."

I grinned at Ella. "Curfew, huh?"

She rolled her eyes. "Yeah. Anyway, I'll see you tomorrow."

With that, she turned and headed inside, leaving me with the unreal vision of her backside as she walked... and the better memory of our kiss as I headed back home, singing Do Wah Diddy Diddy to myself.

# CHAPTER 16

I must have sung Then She Kissed Me two or three times to myself by the time I reached the welcoming light above my home's front door. Still tingling in the memory of Ella's kiss, I was still mouthing the lyrics as I unlocked and entered. Then, aware of the darkness that filled the house, broken by the outside streetlight that filtered inside, I headed to the kitchen for a drink in the gloom.

Dad's bare feet brushed the kitchen floor as he groped his way to the fridge for a drink or snack. At least, that's what I thought, for the fridge light revealed something else.

A stranger's hair, long hair, and feminine curves. Bare...

Her scream filled the kitchen. Mine left my mouth in equal surprise.

Then the kitchen's light switch clicked. Dad shouted something about what was going on, then the woman shouted his name in surprise. Plastic-wrapped cheese slices flopped on the ground as she covered her boobs. I looked away, caught a flash of Dad's dangly bits, and cursed again. I covered my eyes to block their nakedness.

"Jeez! Dad!" I turned away. "I'm sorry. I didn't know." All the happy thoughts of my evening disappeared, leaving me with weird memories of my father which would require future therapy of sorts.

Dad muttered apologies to the woman he called Gloria, and she muttered her own apologies as she bustled to Dad's room. Meanwhile, I stood near the front windows to avoid even one glance that could further scar me.

A moment later, I heard him approach. "Robin?"

I kept looking out the front window at the shadows of the trees on the footpath. Two people walked along the street outside. I hoped they didn't look in my direction.

"Rob?"

"Are you wearing something?" I asked.

"Yeah, yeah," he replied apologetically. "It's okay." I turned to face him, trying not to look down. "See?"

"My eyeballs need scraping. Thanks!"

A grin cracked across his face, erasing the concerned look he had before. Then we started to laugh. He raised a hand to shush me. "She's getting dressed."

"That's your hot date?"

"Yeah, her name's Gloria."

I wanted to say she was pretty, but that might have been inappropriate under the circumstances. From memory, she looked like she was about thirty-eight. Smooth skin. I blinked the memory away because it wasn't cool to remember things like that about my father's girlfriend.

"Are you going to say something?" he asked.

"Sorry to break your fun?"

He shook his head. "You didn't. We were -" he paused as he considered his words "-getting a snack."

I watched in silence. Saying nothing seemed the most appropriate thing. He'd brought no one home before. At least, I didn't think so.

He looked back towards the kitchen, as though checking the coast was clear. "Do you want to have something too?"

I had forgotten my hunger and thirst. Now my stomach rumbled for it. Dad looked at it and grinned. "Come on."

He turned and revealed he was wearing what must have been Gloria's knickers.

"Dressed in a hurry, did you?" I said, stifling a laugh.

"Wouldn't you know it?" He bobbed his hips and bum as he walked like a beach babe off a music video. "Hey, Gloria! It's okay. We're going into the kitchen for a snack. Come on out."

I sat at the table as Dad picked up the cheese slices from the floor and stashed them back in the fridge.

"I know Gloria from work." He grabbed a loaf of bread, butter, and the cheese, dumping them on the table. "Grab some plates, will you?"

"Work?" I repeated. "As in the waterworks?"

"Nah, she works in town hall at the Engineering Department. She's a draftsperson."

"And how'd you meet?"

I took three plates from the cupboard, the same plates I remembered Mum serving our meals on when she was alive. A memory bit at me in tandem with realising Dad was with someone else. Meanwhile he was telling me about how he met her on one of his trips to meet the department head. They'd talked about something or other, blah, blah, blah. He'd met her about eight months ago.

"You've never mentioned her before."

"Sure, I have." He said that quicker than I thought. But I let it slide. Dad wasn't the only one good at keeping secrets. Maybe he thought the same Norman had about Maerie. "I've even dated her a few times when you've been at Norman's place on movie nights."

How many times had Gloria visited? How many times had he visited her place? Then the naked images returned, and I decided not to dwell on it.

At that moment, Gloria stepped in the kitchen. She looked good naked, but she looked great in clothes too... even if it was a pair of denim jeans and t-shirt. With her hair tied back in a ponytail, her cheekbones and educated eyes stood out. Yeah. I knew what Dad saw in her. She looked like Mum had, but blonder.

She gave me a smile, lighting the room, as she offered her hand. "Robin, how are you?"

Her grip was hard when we shook. "Good. Sorry about before, Gloria."

She winked, and I felt her spell work on me. "Don't mention it. I'm sorry if I scared you." Then she looked at the living room and at the kitchen clock. "Weren't you on a date?"

I nodded. "Skating. But she had to be home early."

"That sucks." Empathy filled her voice. "She seems nice."

I gave her a quizzical look and realised she was still

holding my hand, which I took back. "What?"

Dad returned from downstairs, fetching some bottles of cold drink: two beers and a ginger ale. The latter was mine. Gloria afforded him a look.

"Ian! Will you take off my pants?"

Dad responded in surprise. "You mean-?"

Gloria pointed to her red frillies which did little to disguise Dad's lower self. "Get out of my pants."

"Oh."

She giggled. "Not here. Change in the bedroom. Your son's here."

I had to grin at that. Her timing with funny words was great. Dad left and Gloria cracked open her beer.

"What else happened tonight?"

The way she looked at me. It was as if she knew. I hesitated.

"Just tea at the burger joint," I said. "Then we went skating. We left early."

"Why?"

I opened my mouth to answer, and she said, "It's okay. I know something already."

Dad returned. This time he was wearing his stubby shorts and a singlet. He passed his eyes over me, then Gloria, and said, "Did I tell you Gloria's into psychic stuff?" I shook my head. "Let her read your hand. She'll blow your mind."

She already had blown my mind. The tingling feeling from before was like when Maerie looked at me in the hospital. Only this time it was gentler, nicer, kinder. It brushed through my head like a soft breeze, refreshing and cooling. Why did she need to read my hand?

Curious, I held out my hand again. With a gentle touch and disarming smile, she held it. This time, she studied the patterns, tracing a manicured fingernail along them. Now and then, she'd nod, hum to herself, nod again, until at last she gazed into my eyes.

"You've been having nightmares."

Surprised yet sceptical, I glanced at Dad. He shrugged,

pulled a face, and turned to pay attention to the sandwiches he was making. Hiding his guilt, I assumed. I tried to pull my hand back, but Gloria held me still.

"You didn't tell your father about the dreams of the river or the creek, did you?"

With that, Dad dropped the buttered knife on the floor. "What?"

I echoed his surprise. "No. I didn't."

"You're in contact with a thought-form, or some kind of psychic attack."

"Who?"

Gloria released my hand, a tired and worried expression painted on her face, and regarded me. "It's not the spirit of a dead person, Robin," she said. "No. It's..." Her eyes searched the ceiling as though something there would prompt her. Then she shook her head. "No, it can't be that."

"What?"

Then Gloria looked at me. "Years ago, when I was a little older than you, I travelled and read a lot. My journeys took me into India and Tibet, countries that are beautiful, dangerous, and mysterious."

Dad placed a ham and cheese sandwich in front of me, and something that looked like salad without the meat on a sandwich in front of Gloria. He took a bite of his own ham and cheese sandwich.

Gloria watched us eating, and I realised what it was. She was vegetarian.

"While in Tibet, I witnessed things you would expect only to see in movies."

"Like what?" I asked.

She smiled. "Monks whose meditations allowed them to escape gravity. They floated. There were others who meditated to avoid dying. One, it looked like a dried husk of a man, they said was over two hundred years old and still alive. But there was another monk there who... He created things."

I tilted my head. "He was a carpenter?"

She shook her head. "No, he created."

My eyes flicked to Dad, my thoughts a mixture of scepticism and the desire to believe. Recent events, like my strange bleeding the other night, made me wonder. Was this why Dad looked up Gloria again?

Dad realised I was looking at him and glanced back at Gloria.

"What did he create?"

Gloria paused, gazing at both Dad and me before she continued. "Life."

"What?" I couldn't believe my ears. "Life? What kind of life?"

"One night while at the Jokhang Monastery in Lhasa where I spent my retreat, I took a walk outside in Barkhor Square. I usually walked in the late afternoon when things had quietened but I could still observe enough of everyday life. But my studies had taken longer that day, and I could not sleep.

"Outside, everyday life had turned indoors. People were eating their meals late or sleeping or whatever else they did. A blissful quiet filled everything, with only a few animal sounds from cats or dogs in alleyways.

"There in the moonlight sat a monk I had seen but never talked to before. I knew him as Jungney, his name meaning 'the source' or 'origin'. Next to him sat a curious creature with the head and fore-paws of a dog. But it had no hindquarters, the rest of its body elongated like a snake's tail.

"Before I could approach, my teacher Kunchen appeared from nowhere and tapped my shoulder. I turned to face him. He rarely showed emotions other than a smile that crinkled his face and tightened his shaven scalp. But this time, I sensed anger or fear.

"Did you see that, I asked him, and he asked me what I thought I saw. I pointed to Jungney and stopped in surprise. The creature was gone.

"I asked Kunchen to explain. He only shook his head and looked towards Jungney who sat there as though meditating and not noticing."

Gloria took a sip of her beer and watched me in silence for a heartbeat or two.

"What was the creature?"

"I later learned it was a living form of a Tibetan dragon."

"I thought dragons never existed."

Gloria pushed her empty tin to the side and smiled. "They don't. At least not in this reality." Then noticing the unspoken question in my face, she added, "I later learned that Jungney had created the dragon through a rare form of meditation practised by only a few monks."

"Is that because of its difficulty?"

She shook her head. "Because it's hard to control, and one must be a master of many years before attempting it."

"I don't understand."

"Meditation is about focusing one's thoughts. Complete mindfulness of life. To still the mind. When creating a thought-form to a point where others can see, hear, or even feel it, the practitioner must have a still mind free from distractions."

"What happens if you're distracted?"

"Anything can happen."

I thought for a moment about the previous night. Dad looked at me, his eyes looking a little into me as they sometimes did when he studied me. I swear the man knew me better than I did. Then he turned to Gloria. "Like last night?"

Gloria arched an eyebrow at him then turned to me. "Robin, can you tell me about last night's dream?"

So I told her. I told her about the shark, about Louis Patch, and I even mentioned the dream the night before. Dad filled her in on the blood again. And I learned he had already shown her the pictures. All the time, Gloria listened in silence, asking little questions here and there until we had finished.

"This thought-form is close to you. Closer than you think. Do you know of anyone who meditates a lot?"

I shook my head.

"What about interests in Tibetan Buddhism?"

I didn't know anyone like that. "Is anything wrong with Buddhism?"

"No, nothing is wrong with Buddhism. Buddhism is an old philosophy, similar to Christianity, except it is non-violent by nature. There are even scrolls in two monasteries of which I have seen that describe a shining one from the West who visited India to study it nearly two thousand years ago. He later returned from 'the wilderness' to spread the teachings before his crucifixion. Would you say Jesus Christ was wrong?"

My brow crinkled. "He was Buddhist?"

"According to the scrolls, yes, no, maybe. They called him Issa. He taught the same things in parables. The question is not if he studied Buddhism but for how long and how much. The evidence is both historical and textual. But let's stay on track. You have mentioned these dreams, the strange death of this boy, and the bleeding. Is there anything else?"

I thought of the crawling feeling in my head, and Gloria answered her own question.

"You feel sometimes as though someone is in your head."

I nodded.

"Then let's teach you to protect your mind."

# CHAPTER 17

Weird thoughts and dreams danced in my head upon waking the next morning. My brain thumped hard too. A consequence of spending the night talking to Gloria.

One dream was about Maerie. We were living together in it, like a couple. All the time, I kept asking Ella's whereabouts. Maerie kept changing the subject and I stressed myself looking around for her.

In the other, I was hovering over a land I didn't recognise. A large old city spread across the ground, its streets festooned with colourful flags that waved in the breeze. One building, which I guessed to be a monastery, drew my attention and my feet alighted light as a leaf upon the ground before it. Something compelled me to enter between the dragon statues into its darkness.

Upon entering, my surrounding changed, morphed into a large room. The library on Norseman Street in North Middleville. There stood Norman, watching me, a smile on his face. He lifted one of his skinny arms and beckoned with a crooked finger. Entranced, I followed until he at last led me to a shelf of books. He lifted one, showed its title, but my head was foggy. I couldn't read it, but the picture on the front looked strange. It showed a man lying on a bed and another half-image of him floating above it. Again, I tried to read the title. But my head floated, my eyes swam, and I awoke.

The rich aroma of sizzling, greasy bacon and eggs teased my nose. Swallowing the juices from my watering tongue, I sat up, rubbed my head, and trudged out of my room. Giggles form Gloria and Dad's soft laughter reached my ears.

"Is it safe to enter?" I asked, my eyes covered.

"Good morning!" Gloria greeted me with a bright voice. "It's okay. We're decent."

I opened my eyes to see Dad coaxing toast from the toaster; it never popped the pieces anymore. Gloria was watching the stove.

"Do Buddhists eat meat?" I asked her.

She shook her head. "Some do, though it's not normal. I'm happy with my muesli."

"All the more for us," Dad quipped.

I sat down to watch my father and his girlfriend. Something seemed strange about it all. Since Mum died years earlier, he'd not dated a woman. Although unfamiliar to me, Dad's happiness with Gloria warmed me inside. I figured I could adjust to this in time. Gloria brought back to the house what I'd forgotten was missing.

Something caught my eye. A polished black stone shaped like a short obelisk. "What's this?" I asked, running a finger along its smooth obelisk shape. A yin yang symbol crafted in silver glinted in the light.

"Black onyx." Gloria fended away Dad's playful hand with a grin. "Behave." Then she turned her attention back to me. "I believe you could protect yourself with it."

"From what?" I tested the black leather string threaded through the silver attached to the obelisk's base.

"I believe you're receiving psychic attacks from someone. It should help you."

The ends of the leather looked frayed, but its length was enough to tie around my neck. "Thanks."

Gloria helped tie it around my neck. "Have you practised the shielding technique I taught you last night?"

Dad watched as he finished preparing breakfast and dished the eggs and bacon into our plates. His face was placid as a billabong, but happy.

I nodded.

Gloria regarded me for a moment. A sceptical look revealed she saw my lie. "I meant this morning."

"I've just woken."

"Do it before you leave."

I bit my tongue to avoid saying, Yes, Mum. Although my

intention was cheeky, Gloria could have taken it the wrong way. I didn't want to ruin things for Dad if he liked her. Gloria smiled warmly at me and winked.

# CHAPTER 18

Dead on noon, I started work at Hydraworld. It's not there now, but back then it was the place kids went. The cool water and fun attracted kids of all ages: young ones who bobbed about in the shallows; prepubescent and adolescents; older teenagers; and some parents.

A year before, when I first started, the boss delegated me to be Percy Platypus: the mascot. The costume stank of sweat and was heavy. People shouldn't recognise you in it, but it takes one big-mouthed idiot to blab and soon everyone knows. Before long, school chums would call my name while I posed in costume for pictures with kids. I hated it.

This year was different. Another rookie worker had to wear it. Now my job was to keep everything clean and safe. Were the pool noodles and toys safe? Make sure kids didn't run on the wet pool edges.

But that lunchtime, I had to watch the top of the slides: large hollow tubes that spiralled and wound their way to the bottom. Water flowed through them, quicker on some slides which were steeper, and pushed the screaming sliders down to the pool waiting below.

Sometimes an attractive girl would appear, followed by a dozen boys who would jostle to be next in line behind her. This carried benefits for them. They could catch sight of her cute bum and  perv on whatever flesh showed. If they launched down the slide after her, they might "accidentally" touch her in the pool as they fumbled to stand. Then it would start again. Climb to the top, try to be next again, and the playful stalking continued.

Norman and I had tried the same thing once. He claimed he'd felt inside a girl's thigh. But I still don't believe the story.

Being the attendant at the top who watched for safety's sake allowed me to see the whole escapade from another perspective. And when I tried to separate kids from doing the old "let's bunch up and block the tube" trick, they would use the same excuses and cover-ups. The innocent voices with the faces they tried to disguise and deceive. But some of them knew me and my past as a customer. One arched eyebrow and knowing look was all it took to quiet them.

Except for Matthew Stubbs.

I was at the top of the tower, supervising, when I saw him nudging two others. His head tilted conspiratorially while whispering something to them. One guy looked at the entrance to the yellow tube then at me. I pretended not to notice at first as I helped a little kid slide with his young mother. As he took off with a delighted "Whee", I glanced up to see the three bunching together as they watched a distracted attendant.

"Hey, guys," I called. "Only one at a time. No bunching."

They ignored me at first. So I approached. Matthew had his back to me and I tapped him on the shoulder.

He turned his head, his voice's tone already effecting an innocent tone. "What, sir?" Upon the words leaving his mouth, he realised it was me. A sly smirk crossed his face. "What do you want... Robbie?"

"No bunching." My eyes stared into his, like I did on the Tuesday at school.

"Yeah, right." He faced the tunnel again and motioned to the others. "Come on."

My voice deepened with authority. "Wait." I reached forward. The moment I touched his bare shoulder, he screamed and tripped forward so he hit the tube's entrance, his hands stopping the impact.

From my perspective, it was fake. A put-on. But he screamed hard again and shouted. "Leave me alone."

Stunned, I stood there and did nothing. His mates, however, acted quickly and turned to face me.

"Why'd you do that?"

One of them tried pushing me, but his friend stopped him and shook his head.

"Why did you push me?" Matthew turned to me, wincing as though I'd hurt his shoulder. He nursed it with his free hand.

"You leave us alone!" One shouted at me. "He did nothing to you."

I repeated. "Don't bunch up. It's just one at a time."

"You didn't have to push Matthew."

Everything was clear to me then. They had seen me before and this was Matthew's devious trap. And it worked.

At that moment, Eric the boss arrived and heard the shouting and arguing. Eric assessed the situation. He saw the kids crying nearby, soothed by friends or siblings, heard Matthew and his mates bawling me out for something I didn't do, and strode over.

"Stone the bloody crows." His voice was deep, rough. "What's going on here?"

I opened my mouth, but Matthew's was faster.

"He was pushing me around." His finger poked towards me. "I just about hurt my shoulder."

"I didn't," I answered. "He and his mates were bunching up together. I told them to stop."

"He did so push me."

Freckled Freddy (I don't know his real name) nodded. "Yeah. He told us not to bunch, and we said okay. But he had to push Matthew, sir."

To this day, I'm amazed at how we used to call older people Sir or Miss.

Eric's face was red from years of sun exposure. It made him look angry as hell.

Eric looked at me. "Head to the office. I have something for you."

Matthew kept his serious I've-been-done-wrong-by look when Eric turned to him, but I saw his mates suppress smirks. Mission accomplished to them.

I opened my mouth to protest, but Eric shook his head. "Go on."

"This sucks," I muttered under my breath, turned and

headed down the stairs past everyone else's disapproving looks.

As I walked away, I heard Eric telling Matthew to head down the tube. "You two wait." His voice boomed hard. "Wait for him to pass that first bend. Okay. Go. You wait."

I was down the bottom of the stairs when I saw Matthew running fast back from the pool for another go. He stopped when he saw me, my fist balled with anger. The smile on his face faded when he turned back towards the pool. My guess is he was looking for someone else. More than likely, he would change the story again.

I waited outside Eric's office, a tiny shed filled with other pool toys. Percy the Platypus' huge head sat on a nearby table and grinned back at me as though he knew everything would be okay. But I wasn't sure. Eric had a good head on his shoulders, was even an old mate of my father, but I didn't know.

His voice surprised me and I turned.

"What's going on?" Eric asked.

"I already told you."

"That fat kid tells me you bailed him up again at the stairs."

I shook my head. "I saw him. He saw me. But we didn't speak or do anything. He went to the pool."

Eric nodded in understanding. "I don't trust that little shit. He's just like his bloody father. Manipulative bastards like him grow to become big people with influence. Some change for the better; the others never change and continue as users." He winked and smiled as his fingers rolled a cigarette and pinched the end. "Watch out for that kid, Robin. Boys like him, the so-called popular ones, can grow up to be users. They'll suck people dry like a can of beer and toss them like an empty. Don't be one of them."

"So you knew he lied?"

He chuckled. "I wasn't born in the last shower."

"Then why get up me in front of him and the others?"

"Have a seat." Eric motioned to an upended plastic box,

while he found another for himself, the unlit cigarette dangling from his mouth. "I didn't tell you off in front of everyone. I removed you from the situation. Sometimes it's best not to enter the fight. Let them think they've won. What those little snots think isn't the truth until you believe it yourself."

The whole thing sounded like bull to me. But I appreciated one thing. Eric knew Matthew was full of shit. That was good enough for me.

"Is that it?"

"Yeah. Besides, Malcolm saw the whole thing. I got those boys down the tube so I could talk to him without their pestering shit. Malcolm said the same as you. Doesn't that mean something to you?"

Yeah. I had to agree with Eric's logic on that.

"Malcolm up there. So's Ray. Any more crap from them, and they're out for the day."

For a while, I sat there, not knowing what to do. Eric lit up a cigarette and took a drag before letting the smoke billow from his nose. With the red face, he looked like an angry cartoon bull - without the nose ring.

He turned to me again. "Aren't you supposed to be working?"

"Are we done?"

"Yeah, sport. Go help at the canteen. Hopefully, the fat poofy kid isn't hungry yet."

A grin crossed my face at how he referred to Matthew. I'd always thought the same since second grade, but Eric was the first to say it.

"Well, hurry up! Don't stand there with doe-eyes. Go!"

His merry chuckle reached my ears as I headed to the canteen with a lighter heart.

The rest of the work day flew. It's incredible how time shrinks and stretches according to our moods and activity.

It was so busy, I served so many hot chips with tomato sauce to customers that I didn't realise the time until Grace asked me what time I finished.

"Five," I told her.

"It's quarter past six now," she said. And she smiled. "You've got someone waiting for you."

I followed the direction in which she pointed, and the warm fuzzies danced over my body at the sight of Ella. There she stood, dressed in a yellow one-piece that contrasted with her tanned skin, beach towel wrapped around her waist. Picture postcard perfect. My mind drifted back to the night before with the kiss.

"Well, go on! Don't keep the young lady waiting." Grace winked. "I'll tell Eric about how you helped overtime. Have fun."

I removed my apron and handed it to her as I left the canteen and hurried to meet Ella.

Ella waved as I approached and gave me a hug. She was the first person outside my family who I had hugged. And knowing she was in a Speedo swimsuit made the moment more delicious. She looked up and smiled into my face. "How was your day?"

"Not bad," I said. "Better now. And you?"

"Great."

Then I saw her backpack at her feet. "Do you want to keep that with mine in the staff locker?"

She said she did. After stowing it away with mine, I changed into my togs, and soon after we climbed the towers to try a slide.

With the water swooshing around her feet at the top, I asked her if she'd visited the slide at night before. Ella shook her head. "Then you will love this." I gave her a choice of the three coloured slides: yellow, brown, or blue. She chose blue, and I suggested she leave that one for last. "You'll see why."

Ella changed her first choice to yellow, which was the longest slide, and went before me. Although she had the head-start, I knew how to slide smoother and faster so I soon caught up to her. Her scream of laughter echoed off the tube's walls and mixed with the gentle sound of the rushing water. And the tube's interior glowed a pale golden light. At last, we splashed down into the pool at the end. The second tube, brindle brown, was fun but nowhere near as good as the first.

"Now the blue," I said, leading Ella up the stairs again.

There's a reason I suggested Ella leave the blue tube for last. Yes, it was my favourite. Through the day it was fun, even as the fastest, but there was more. Being summer, the water was cool, but the friction on the tube as we slid down made it feel warmer. The blue light that filtered into the translucent tube from the outside floodlights made the experience heavenly. A mixture of lighter blue, darker at the joins, flicked and swirled as the current pushed us along. The only problem: the moment passed too soon before we splashed into the pool.

Like the other boys who jostled to catch up to the hot girls at the tower top, so they could touch her in the pool, I wanted to do the same to Ella. It wasn't difficult as she slammed into me upon her own entry into the water. When we both caught our breaths above the surface, Ella was beaming. Light reflected from her wet face and emphasised her features.

"How'd you enjoy that?"

"I loved it! It was like flying through a rainy sky."

Points for me.

We slid a few more times before we realised our stomachs grumbled for food. Ella didn't feel like chips from the canteen, and neither did I. After working in there for the afternoon, the last place I wanted was to eat at work. So after drying off and changing clothes, we headed to the burger joint next door for a quick bite. Conversation was easy, easier than when I used to just look at Ella before and struggle to find words. Now we talked about our interests, what we would like to do on holidays. It was as if nothing else mattered in the world but us and our hopes and dreams. Then we decided it was time to head home.

But this time, she asked if it was okay to stop at my place this time. Ella's tone was quieter, focused, and I realised

something else sat in her mind.
"We need to talk."

# CHAPTER 19

We need to talk.

The words sent tremors through my spine like listening to a teacher scrape their fingernails down a blackboard. I knew from listening to other guys that those words meant the girl wanted to break the relationship. Little balls of panic and trepidation filled my stomach and lodged in my gut.

"We need to talk?" I allowed the words to hang in the air for her.

"Yeah." That's all she said.

The walk home seemed longer than usual. Questions raced through my mind as I wondered. Was it something I'd done? What about another chance? Breaking up with Ella would prove awkward. What if she broke up with me then Norman woke? How could I face him?

"Why are you so quiet?" Ella's eyes searched mine as we waited at the traffic lights again. "You haven't said a thing the whole time."

"I'm wondering why you want to break up."

"Break up?" Her brow furrowed. "What are you talking about? Where did you get that idea?"

I shrugged. "You said we had to talk. Isn't that code for you wanting to break up?"

She laughed. "You dag! No. I meant we have to talk. You remember, don't you? The whole thing with Wednesday Addams?"

Wednesday Addams? "Oh, you mean Maerie?"

"Yes!"

A huge grin crossed my face, accompanied by the bright burning sensation of an embarrassed blush blooming. "Oops."

She laughed again. I loved her laugh. It was genuine, not the insincere plastic some make. "No. You're funny."

At last, we reached my house. It must have been eight o'clock. The lights were still on, which pleased me, and I hoped to myself that Dad and Gloria were clothed.

As a precaution, I called out as we came in. "Dad, I'm home. Ella's with me."

Dad answered from the lounge-room. "We're in here." A slight pause. "Hang on, I'll get my -"

Gloria's voice interrupted him. "Stop teasing. Everything's okay, Robin." She admonished him but I couldn't catch the words in her harsh whispers.

Dad stood up from the double sofa where Gloria remained seated. "Have a seat, Ella. We didn't know you were stopping by."

Ella replied to Dad, and he introduced her to Gloria who stood to give her a large hug.

"Robin mentioned you," Ella said.

Gloria gave her a gracious smile, glanced at me and said, "He didn't tell you everything, did he?"

"He said enough." Ella allowed her voice to hang on the last word.

A stunned silence sat in the air between them. Gloria's eyes studied Ella's who remained poker-faced until they both laughed at the obvious joke between them.

Gloria giggled as she told me she liked Ella. "Keep him on his toes, Ella."

My Dad and Gloria excused themselves from the living room and headed out the back. I breathed a sigh of relief that they hadn't retired to the bedroom. The previous night was the first time I'd heard nocturnal mating habits. Those sounds wouldn't be cool with visitors.

Ella sat on the large sofa and leaned back in a stretch. Then she looked at me, eyebrow arched. "Were you perving at my boobs?"

I shrugged. "The way they poked out at me through your shirt, how could I not?"

She grinned. "Good to know."

"You said we should talk."

Ella hummed. "Yeah. Norman received a letter yesterday from the town library." She reached for her backpack, opened it, and removed some books. Library books. "He must have been riding to the library when he had the accident. He didn't arrive to return them, so we have the overdue letter."

"Is this them?"

The cover of one showed a woman with fingers raised to her temples, her eyes half-closed as though meditating or trancing. To me, it looked like she had a nasty headache. Its title was large enough to shout: Mysteries Of The Mind. Another book had a cover picture of a man lying on a bed, and above him, a ghostly duplicate floated: Astral Travelling For Beginners.

"Looks like he was studying some heavy stuff."

"Mind-reading, maybe?" Ella guessed. "Does that sound familiar?"

Flashes of the previous night came to mind: Ella's supposition about vampires; Maerie's knack for being around at odd times and knowing things.

"Maybe. But I still don't think she's a vampire."

"A witch?" Ella guessed. "If he was reading this stuff when she met him at the library, it could have led to a conversation."

"Or maybe he borrowed them because he saw her reading similar things."

My mind drifted to another time when both Norman and I visited the library together. I was borrowing Bill Cosby cassettes. He was looking at two other girls when they walked past us giggling. They weren't bad looking either, and Norman wanted us to follow them. I was the wingman. It didn't work.

"What were you thinking?" Ella asked.

I shook my head. "Just wondering what else is in the books."

"There were more books." Ella placed the first two aside and showed me another one. "They still have bookmarks in them. I think he was going to re-borrow them."

"Taking notes," I murmured, picking up one with the picture of a man dressed in robes on the front of it. Tibetan Mysteries. Memory of Gloria's tale returned to me. "Have you looked at the pages he marked?"

Ella nodded, flicking through the Mysteries of the Mind book. "Yeah, I had a quick look but haven't read it all. There's some weird shit here." She pointed to a page marked by a torn piece of notepaper that served as a mark. "Check this part."

I took the hardcover book and skimmed the writing. Then a few words demanded my thorough attention and urged me to read properly. They told of a group of a Dr Owen, a mathematician, and a psychologist Dr Joel Whitton who oversaw an experiment in thought projection. With a group of students, they created a fictional character named Philip Aylesford who was alive in the 1600s. Parts of his history coincided with real-life events such as a Civil War and he was a spy for King Charles II. A Gypsy girl he loved was tried and executed for witchcraft, which led to his suicide. Together, the students attempted to talk to the fictional character through seances. At first, they were unsuccessful. They tried different things, even started joking around. And that's when things got hairy. A table moved. Two raps sounded in different places. Soon they were conversing through sounds. This all happened in 1972, even on television, the chapter said.

Awed, I glanced up at Ella. "Is this saying what I think it is?"

Ella nodded. "They created a ghost."

"Far canal," I muttered, the tension popping from my forehead. "But wait a minute. Are you saying that -"

Ella shook her head. "I'm not saying anything, but can you see a parallel happening here?"

I shut the book with a thump. "This isn't right. It can't be. We can see her. Maerie is real."

"Real weird, yes."

"Do you believe it?"

Ella nodded. "At first, I didn't. But when I think about everything, I do."

Something came to mind. Gloria's tale of the monk who created the furry dragon. It sounded like it came from NeverEnding Story, but what if it was true? I grabbed the Tibetan Mysteries book and looked for another bookmark. Yep, there it was. Another torn piece of notepaper marking the middle of the book.

"Have you read this one?"

Ella shook her head.

I opened it and scanned through the passages, and each word fit together in the puzzle.

"What is it?" Ella asked.

I shook my head. "Hang on. I'm reading it."

"I know. Your lips are moving. What's it say?"

"This part is about a lady called Teal David-Neel. She studied Buddhism and travelled throughout Tibet in her studies."

"And?"

"She created a thought-form, based on her own fantasies of a monk who resembled Friar Tuck. At first, only she could see him. Then she could feel his touch. Others could see, hear and feel him too."

Ella's eyes widened, her mouth open in disbelief. "Shit!"

She grabbed the book and turned it around to read the paragraphs I pointed for her. Her eyes flicked back and forth as she studied the paragraphs.

"He created his own girlfriend by meditating on her."

I didn't want to ask, but I had to do it. "Did you see a journal or diary Norman kept?"

She shook her head. "I know he kept one. He sometimes stayed up late to write about his day." A laugh escaped her lips. "I once took it from him and threatened to show a girl what he wrote about her. He cried, so I gave it back."

"Why did you do that?"

"He took too long in the bathroom when I wanted to

shower."

I gave a short laugh. "Back to this, what do you think about this one in Tibet?"

"Everything adds up," Ella nodded, "but are we reading too much into this?"

"Gloria told me a similar story about herself. She travelled to Tibet too."

Ella tilted her head with interest. "Did she create one?"

"No. Another monk there did. And she saw it. A tiny dragon. But her own teacher hustled her away. It's as if the practice is taboo or something."

"The Neal lady's tulpa turned nasty."

"I missed that part."

"You should have kept reading." Ella pointed to the text. "See? It turned gaunt, sinister-looking, and the people who saw it became worried."

"That's not exactly nasty," I answered.

"No, but they must have had reason to fear it. Think about how Maerie beat up Paul and Jason last night."

Then my dream of Grants Creek came to mind. Lou Patch and the girl.

"Do you think Maerie shares Norman's hatred of those who bullied him? Jason, Paul, Matthew... Louis Patch?"

"What about Louis Patch?"

I told her about my dream and reminded her about how the dream happened the night he died. Her mouth dropped open, a grotesque caricature of Luna Park's entrance.

"No way."

"Yes way," I responded. "And what about the episodes where we feel her in our heads? What if she is a thought-form, and being a creature of thought she can read our minds?"

"She does."

I reached around my neck, removed the protection stone Gloria gave me. "I'd like you to have this."

"That's beautiful," she said, watching the light reflect from its polished surface. "What is it?"

"It's for protection. Gloria gave it to me to protect against psychic attacks--keep people out of your head. I want you to have it." Taking the amulet, I tied it around her neck.

"Thanks," she said. A suspicious look crossed her face. "Is there something more to this? Why don't you keep it and protect yourself?"

I shrugged. "Gloria has been teaching me other ways to protect myself. I want you to have it."

I didn't tell her it was because of the nightmare I had before I woke with blood streaming from my face. Perhaps I should have. I didn't want to worry her.

# CHAPTER 20

TEENAGERS DEAD IN POOL

The newspaper's front page screamed the words.

I rarely read the paper. Sensational headlines bore me and, on occasion, depress me. Even in those days. Usually I would read the sports and the comics - The Phantom, Swamp, Footrot Flats and Garfield. But Louis Patch's death remained fresh in my mind and that inflamed my curiosity more.

The story described two as yet unnamed teenage boys found on Saturday morning dead in the waters of Central Park's fountains. Rumours were the park was the meeting place for certain groups of men, young and old, who would meet for "backdoor activity". I had heard the stories before and wondered how true they were. The park was on George Street, the main entry and exit point for Middleville's south side to the Central Highway leading towards Brisbane. The next street that sandwiched the park was Murray Street with Central Park Motel facing it.

"I heard they found a chewed-up cock in the arse of one of them." I turned towards the familiar voice. Randall Seppings, dressed ready for work at his father's business, nodded at me. "It's Jason Baker and Paul Thornton. I didn't even know they were poo-pokers."

"Really?" I scanned the story which continued on page 3.

He snorted. "It doesn't mention names, but you know how word travels."

"Fast enough to make Dick Johnson look like he's driving in reverse." I found mention in the story of a 'foreign object' lodged in one victim's rectum. "It doesn't mention what the thing is, but it might be true."

"Funny that, eh?" Randall paid the newsagent for the paper and headed out the door. "Catch you around the S-bend, mate. Gotta go."

I dropped my payment for the paper and my Phantom comic in the shopkeeper's hand and left too. The walk home along Main Street went quicker than expected. As I scanned the story, I remembered why I hated reading the paper. It described more than a foreign object. Whoever killed Jason and Paul had decapitated one of them and thrown the head onto Murray Street. A motorist found it in their car's headlight beams at 2am Saturday morning.

I thought for a moment. I had worked Saturday. No one mentioned any deaths. Sometimes news travelled slower than a sloth in Middleville. Then I saw the other story.

SECURITY GUARD INJURED AT SKATING RINK

This grabbed my attention because I was there. The report detailed how the security guard had suffered a mental breakdown. Straight after talking to a group of teenagers about a scuffle, he walked to the toilet where he abused himself with a toilet brush. The article didn't mention names. It was all sensation with no substance. But for anyone who knew that two of the teenagers involved in the scuffle also appeared in the front-page story, it screamed the truth.

# CHAPTER 21

Every December, since Mum and my sister died, Dad obtained annual leave to coincide with my summer holidays and Christmastime. The Council waterworks had Christmas shifts to ensure the city's water supply and quality, meaning he had to apply for the leave and not expect Christmas Day off.

On the first day of annual leave, 8th of December 1986, he slept in. What I didn't know is if Gloria was at work or in the bedroom with him. I wondered.

Part of me still winced at how long he had known Gloria without mentioning her to me. Not that I told Dad everything about my new love life. There wasn't much to tell. That was different, though it was good to see him happy again. Until she stopped by, I couldn't remember Dad being so happy.

Dropping the newspaper on the kitchen table for Dad to find, I thought about the rest of the day. Ella was going to the library in the morning to drop off Norman's overdue books. The way we pored over them on the Saturday night made me wonder if Ella might re-borrow them herself. I'd never seen someone so absorbed by a subject, almost obsessive. She was busy on Sunday and seeing one of her friends who lived near Oasis Gardens, not far from school. And she visited Norman again. I would have seen Norman, too, if I didn't have to mow the lawn. I'd be seeing them both that afternoon after lunch.

That meant I'd likely see Maerie. The thought of the strange tickling and poking sensations in my head gave me the shivers. So I decided to practise again the technique Gloria taught me: psychic protection.

Gloria had told me a couple of techniques to create what she called a psychic shield.

One was what she called The Bubble. It involved visualising a large bubble around myself. The bubble, she said, would be like a transparent rubber wall that only I could see. It worked best by imagining someone run at me, hit the wall, and bounce away. That seemed ridiculous to me, which paradoxically made it easier to imagine — but not to believe. When Gloria asked why the idea challenged me, I asked why the bubble didn't break. Such a patient woman, she replied that it repelled negative energy and psychic attacks. "But I don't know if it will work," I had said. "For you," she told me, "it will be natural. You're a dream walker." That was the second time someone mentioned that to me. What did it mean? Gloria said it meant something about leaving my body to see things in the world around me. It meant I could visualise things enough to visit or see them. Such an ability indicated I could easily create a psychic bubble.

I liked the idea of the bubble. It was easier than imagining myself in a ball, similar to the bubble, but consisting of lots of mirrors to reflect away. It made me think of a disco ball. Somehow, thinking of a bouncy bubble was easier.

It would have to do.

But would it pass the test?

# CHAPTER 22

Confidence fortified my thoughts as I strode along the hospital corridors towards Norman's room. The bubble enclosed me, staying just two centimetres away from my body to allow a stretch if something touched it. That way, I would be aware of the negative presence without it harming me. At least, that was my plan. Upon recognising my dark thought, I mentally kicked it out of the shield. Negativity was not allowed inside my barrier in case it rotted me from inside.

As expected, three of them waited in the room with Norman: Ella, her mother, and Maerie.

A curious, distant look inhabited Mrs Cole's face as though she was no longer mentally present. Her mouth gaped open like her vacant eyes as she gazed at Norman. Maerie's own gaze bore at Ella in deep concentration while Ella looked back in open defiance.

"What's going on here?"

Maerie whipped her gaze towards me, her eyebrows arched in surprise. "Robin!" Lines of confusion flickered across her forehead for an instant before melting to nothing. "How long have you been here?"

"Just now."

I allowed a smile to cross my face as I took a chair and sat between Ella and Maerie. Mrs Cole's face remained the same - a sideshow clown, mouth opened wide to catch flies.

"Mrs Cole? Is everything okay?"

"She's been like that since Maerie arrived." Ella glared at Maerie. "You were about to say something, Maerie."

My vision wobbled slightly a moment. Ripples passed before my eyes, making the room appear to shake like jelly. I could guess why. Maerie's familiar hard stare greeted me when I turned to face her.

"What's happening?"

Her studious eyes regarded me, the colours as deep as her namesake. "You appear different today, Robin. What is it? A new cologne?"

More interested in Mrs Cole's predicament, I ignored Maerie's apparent ploy. "Have you called the nurses? Mrs Cole looks like she's had a stroke. Look at her mouth."

"They're not coming," Ella answered, her voice a whisper. "And Maerie has something to say."

Maybe a coffee would have helped that morning. How could I miss that? "Did you do this, Maerie?"

Maerie's composure remained still and steady and I realised she was studying me like a crocodile lying in wait. The ripples and prods continued, and I could just sense the sound of something tapping on the bubble's wall. Before long, Maerie's mouth opened in a wide smile of realisation. "A shield!"

Ella flinched at the mention. Maybe I did too. I didn't want to.

"What do you mean?" Perhaps Maerie realised my bluff. "You placed a shield across your mind. Interesting." Her gaze came back to Ella. "And you too. Are you my enemies?"

It wasn't worth pretending now. "Enemies?" I straightened, visualising a cloud of white light to appear around Ella and me. Maybe I concentrated too long because I could have sworn twenty seconds passed before I continued. "Why? Should we be concerned about you?"

"So you are concerned about me?" Maerie sounded incredulous, her voice melting butter in her mouth. "I am Norman's girlfriend. Any friends of his are mine. And so are his family."

Ella responded to the white light and its effect upon her. Although the onyx I gave her provided protection, the extra positivity from my white bubble fortified her. Confidence returned to her voice. "Yet you bewitched Norman's mother. My mother. Why?"

Maerie shrugged. "She is Norman's mother, not his mistress. She cares for his welfare, but she cares more for how things reflect on her. Selfish, but I still love her as Norman's mother."

"Love?" I asked with a laugh. "Is it right to control those you love?"

"You never asked her the same thing about Norman." Maerie looked between Ella and me. "I asked if your shield means you don't like me? What are you hiding?"

"Even family and friends have a right to privacy."

"You sound tense."

It was a ploy which I ignored.

"What have you done to Norman's mother?" I countered. "She needs help."

Maerie turned to look at Mrs Cole whose chin grew a string of drool that stretched towards her lap and dripped into it. Ella reached forward with a Kleenex to catch and wipe it away from Mrs Cole's dress. "Is she aware of what we're saying?"

Maerie didn't answer. Instead, she watched Mrs Cole for a while longer. Her silence unsettled us.

"Well?" I asked. "Is she?"

The strange girl turned to look at me. Again, the bubble twitched. I guessed the tulpa was attempting to invade my mind and thoughts but said nothing. "How long do you think your bubble will keep me out?"

A smile crossed her face when I flinched at her words.

Something caught my eye. I dropped my gaze towards Maerie's throat to see a shark's tooth. A memory flickered. I squinted my eyes, examined the piece closer, and gasped in surprise. "Louis Patch."

Maerie's hand reached towards the tooth and fondled it, her fingertip playing with its sharp point. A smile of recognition. "Yes. He gave it to me."

"You killed Louis." I should have guessed it sooner. Maybe I had, but I didn't have the proof.

"Of course."

"Why?"

"Because I am loyal to Norman. Patch hurt Norman. I

couldn't stop him before, but I could stop him doing it again." A look of horror and disgust crossed Ella's face. "How did you kill him?"

Maerie opened her mouth to speak, but I interrupted. "She bonked him at Grants Creek right before she impaled him in a tree."

Maerie's eyes widened. She squinted her eyes at me again. The bubble shimmered around me, wobbled with each psychic blow she dealt my shield. "How could you know that?"

She stopped a moment to consider. Then a smile slowly appeared on her face, laced with cunning. "You were there."

"And you had it off with Louis Patch," I added. "Is that being faithful to Norman?"

The tulpa flinched for just a moment. "The end justified the means."

"And what of Jason and Paul?" I pushed hard on the point. "Did you bonk them too?"

"Does it matter?"

"For one who claims loyalty to Norman, it should. What does he think about it?"

She shrugged indifferently. "They hurt Norman. And they attacked you and Ella. I chose to stop them because you're Norman's friend."

"What?" Ella's face paled and she shook her head. "By killing them? That was unnecessary."

Maerie leaned over Norman's comatose self to kiss his sleeping lips. The poor guy. Had Norman been aware of her kiss, what did he think of Maerie's murderous actions? Did he enjoy the kiss she lovingly bestowed upon him, sucking his bottom lip before parting? Only they knew.

Ella pulled a face as she watched the exchange and looked away. Although a disgust of sorts filled me, knowing Maerie's general origin and her actions, it was impossible not to watch.

At last, Maerie lifted herself to her full height, the hint of a gloat in her visage. Long fingers smoothed a trail down her dress and over her shapely hips and thighs that showed through the material. "Robin." Thick vocal honey flowed from the vixen's lips as she spoke. "I need your help with the rest of the boys."

"You've got to be joking," I answered, resisting her voice and barely keeping my psychic shield. "Why would I help you kill others?"

Maerie cocked her head to the side, one hand resting on her hip while the lifted and clicked its fingers. In that moment, Mrs Cole moved. I nearly missed it; she was so fast as she reached towards Ella. A pair of scissors lashed forward and snipped through the leather string around Ella's neck. The onyx clattered on the floor, my confidence with it. Maerie kicked it away towards the adjoining bathroom.

Before I could wonder where Mrs Cole found the large scissors, her hand had grabbed Ella's head back by her hair; the other held the blade's to her trembling throat. A tiny frightened cry escaped Ella's lips.

"It's an offer you can't resist." Maerie's smile exuded triumph as she turned to me. "Submit or she dies."

# CHAPTER 23

Panic filled my head. My psychic shield popped and crumbled at the unexpected turn of events. Almost instantly, Maerie's mental fingers passed through my consciousness. I felt them rifle through my thoughts and memories as though searching a filing cabinet.

Tears streaked Ella's face as she watched me, a pained expression in her eyes. She dared move ever so slightly to shake her head. "No," her mouth mimed. Her mother's scissors pressed into her skin, the indent frightening me more.

Maerie's voice echoed through my mind as though she were inside it, searching through those mental cabinets. Finished with one, she slammed it shut with an exasperated sigh and started searching through another. "Did you think you would hold me off forever? A creature of thought."

A memory of Norman and I as kids playing Army flickered as though Maerie played it from an 8 mm film projector. An exasperated cry rattled through my mind again. Another memory flashed; the time Norman and I hid under the teacher's desk in first grade, and we saw up Skye Cassidy's skirt. It faded. Maerie slammed another memory in my head as though with mental fists. "I was born from thoughts and memories."

Then another flashback flickered; colourful flags fluttering in a breeze outside a monastery. The memory was so old, it was foreign to me. What was it? Then the warm, coppery tang of blood filled my mouth. I gagged. Meanwhile, Maerie continued her search in my head. For what? "With a single thought, he created me."

At last, Maerie relaxed her ferocious search long enough to study my eyes. A knowing look crossed her visage as she did. "You lied about seeing Louis Patch's death"

I remained still, placid, thinking of my Dad, wondering what wisdom he would say about this. But none came.

Maerie stepped away from me, glided along the floor back to Norman's side. "Yes, you saw me and Louis. But you didn't see me kill him. Neither did you see he and I bonk. You lied."

"Yet you admitted to it." My calmness surprised me. Part of me believed my death would come soon. Fearing the inevitable is pointless.

"It matters not. I have found what I need... for now."

I noticed the EEG printer beside Norman's bed. Its pen scribbled back and forth with the same rapidity I'd witnessed upon Maerie's first appearance. But this time, the wavelengths seemed different. What did it mean?

Maerie must have noticed the difference too. For a moment, she was distracted by the movements of the EEG's plotter before gazing back at Norman's sleeping form. Something moved. Was it a finger twitch? Then it stopped, and the EEG resumed its leisurely curves.

"Everything I do, I do for you, Norman." Maerie's voice was firm, but I could have sworn it trembled slightly. "You may not understand it. But in time, you will." She squeezed Norman's pale hand in hers with tenderness, gazing at him.

And with that, she vanished.

# CHAPTER 24

Until Maerie vanished, I hadn't understood the extent of Maerie's presence and how it affected us.

Upon her disappearance, sounds permeated from the hallway outside. The orderlies and hospital staff's chatter, other visitors walking past the door, and the occasional ding of a bedside buzzer calling the nurses. It was like the building sprang back to consciousness. It happened in the room, too, for the scissors clattered to the floor from Mrs Cole's fingers as they dropped to her side. Then her eyes flickered as though awakening from a mad dream.

"My word! I must have dropped off."

She wiped drool from her mouth and regarded it with mild confusion. Then like a cat that pretends it hadn't fallen from a table and created a mess, she casually searched through her purse.

Then she saw me. "Oh, Robin! I didn't see you there." Masked confusion made her look around. "How long was I asleep?"

"Not long," I lied, giving Ella a warning look to remain quiet about what happened. Her hands trembled slightly, their skin pale as her face from shock.

Mrs Cole then noticed the wet patch on the front of her royal blue dress. After a moment's hesitation, she stood, excusing herself as she passed me on the way to the en-suite to wash.

"You really are becoming a regular at the hospital, Robin," Mrs Cole said above the running water in the en-suite's basin. "It's almost like you're a member of the family. Maerie is, too. Such a lovely girl."

Ella and I exchanged knowing glances as Mrs Cole continued her monologue. Her mother emerged from the en-suite, wiping her hands on a paper towel, when something caught her eye. She bent down and dangled the object to squint at it. "Ella, isn't this your necklace?"

"Yes, it is." Ella's voice appeared surprised, but I caught the effected tone. The horror of Maerie's confrontation obviously lingered in her mind as much as mine. It added to the tonality. "How did it get there?" She held out her hand and took it from Mrs Cole. "Oh, the string's broken."

"Better keep it safe," Mrs Cole said, giving me a small wink. "Robin might think you don't appreciate the gift."

Ella pushed the stone into her jeans pocket as I gave a half-knowing wink to her.

Mrs Cole smacked her lips and screwed up her face. "My mouth is dry. I'll go buy a drink. Do you kids want anything?"

We each shook our head as Mrs Cole retrieved her purse and headed towards the door. "See you soon."

Once alone, Ella let out a sigh. I hurried to her, holding her tight and close, as she gripped me tight. The tension of the past quarter hour still lingered in our limbs.

"I thought I was going to lose you," Ella whispered.

"Me too." My fingers tangled in her locks as I held her close. "The way your mother--"

I stopped my words. We were in enough shock without deliberately reliving the horror. Ella trembled against me as we rocked back and forth. All the time, I kept whispering the mantra: everything's okay; you're safe.

"I can hear your thumping heart," Ella said, lifting her head a few beats later to look in my face. She kissed my lips. Fear and worry made it taste extra special. "What did Maerie do to you?"

I shook my head. "I think she searched my memories." I explained the feeling. How I thought Maerie was looking for something in particular. For what, I didn't know. "What about you?"

Ella shook her head. "The stone protected me until Mum cut it, but even without it, Maerie didn't try my memories like before. Whatever she wanted, she wanted it from you." She looked up at me. "Do you still think there's nothing about Maerie?"

I placed a finger to my lips, pointed at Norman, and mimed his name to Ella. "What matters is we're safe. For now." It was difficult, but I pulled away from Ella's arms long enough to reach into my backpack and remove the Walkman and headphones.

At the moment I placed the headphones over his ears, Norman's finger twitched. I damn near jumped. It was like viewing a corpse in a morgue and learning it wasn't really dead.

But there were no more twitches.

Norman still looked so alien without his black-framed glasses. He'd had different versions of the same frames for so long, like a die-hard Buddy Holly fan. What was going on behind his closed eyelids?

"Do you think he's aware of everything we do and say?"

Ella shrugged, her eyes studying her brother. She paused, words stuck on the edge of her lips like a hesitant cliff diver. I nodded to confirm the music was playing in Norman's ears. "I wonder if Maerie's attacks are what he wants."

"What? No way. He's your brother."

Ella pointed at her sleeping brother. "I once dreamed I was kissing another girl," she said. "And it was good." She laughed. "No, I don't mean like that. I'm definitely not a lezzo." She took a deep breath and collected her words. "It's the sort of fantasy dream where you know it's against your personal values. You wouldn't do it in real life, but you live it in a dream... even if you feel guilty and want to wake from it."

"Do you mean the kind where I might dream of robbing a bank, yet I wouldn't do it in real life?"

"Yes! Exactly." Ella's face lit at my understanding and gestured towards Norman. "Maybe his dreams are influencing Maerie."

I paused to think. The idea shocked me and added to the recent dread.

"That could be dangerous, if it's true." I sat close to Norman as I considered Ella's theory. "Do you think he's asked Maerie to kill them? They were the most dangerous ones."

"Maybe."

"What happens if he gets angry with us about something in his dreams?"

The idea silenced us so the only sounds in the room came from the EEG plotter and the wall clock's ticking. Dad's words from Saturday returned to me. There's something about Norman, and it's not right. Meanwhile, Norman slept, his face still as a blind man's face, but was he listening through the music playing in his ears?

I looked up at Ella who was watching from the foot of Norman's bed and shook my head. "No. I don't believe it. Maerie acts on her own."

"How can you be sure?"

"Do you remember how she looked at Norman before? She looked like she wanted to please him."

Ella allowed a smile. "She loves him."

"Well, he is your brother." I grinned. "But seriously, it made me think of someone who would do anything to please the person they love. Loyalty. Fanatical loyalty. Like an animal so angry to see someone kill its mother, they would do the same in return."

"So are we safe?"

"We haven't hurt Norman," I answered with a nod. "But Louis Patch did. And Jason and Paul did too." I took a breath to think, and the other idea hit me. "Oh, shit."

"What?"

"What happens when she's run out of people to kill?"

At that moment, Mrs Cole returned, slurping on a plastic bottle of Orchy orange juice from a paper straw. The conversation changed, turned to small talk and moments of awkward silence as Ella and I struggled to find other things to say. So much is forgotten when one is stuck with the terrible question: who is Maerie's next target?

# CHAPTER 25

By the time I arrived home from the hospital, I was a nervous wreck. Even today, I shudder at the memory of that day. Thoughts flooded my head, and my mind screamed for peace. I wanted to be alone, to think and process. The ride home helped, but it wasn't enough.

When I finally reached home on my bike, Gloria was just arriving from round the corner. She must have caught a bus, I figured. At the sound of my dinging bell, she turned, her blonde hair waving in the breeze as she waved to me.

"Robin," she called, still approaching as I pulled into my driveway. "How was your day?"

It's funny. When asked how we are, our first answer is, "Good", even if we're not. Chaos and turmoil raged in my mind, mixed with fear. My answer?

"Pretty good."

Gloria said nothing. Just studied me. Her eyes flicked to my shoulders and looked a little to the left of my face.

"Your aura is greyer."

I summoned every bit of my inner resolve, forced a happy expression on my face, as we walked alongside each other to the house. Meanwhile, she continued gazing at me. A tiny flutter of something touched inside my thoughts. Gloria's psychic fingers, I guessed. Yet I flinched.

Gloria's soft voice soothed. "Robin, what happened?"

"The stone didn't work."

Gloria's eyebrow arched and the late afternoon sun glinted from her eye. "I see you're not wearing it. What happened?"

Like water from a broken tap, the words tumbled from my mouth. As I relayed the story, Gloria merely listened, occasionally asking a question and key points, until I finished.

"The shield worked then, and so did the stone."

"But it didn't." My voice cracked in frustration. "Mrs Cole cut the string. Ella could have--"

"Ella lived, Robin." Gloria's voice carried serenity. "Be thankful for the good that happened and the bad that didn't." Her eyes looked into mine, and she gave a short nod. "Yeah?"

I took a breath. "Yeah."

"Maerie merely changed her strategy," Gloria said, her voice trailing slightly. "She's cunning. Smart."

I hung the bike from the hooks in the wall under the house. "Is that normal for a Tulpa?"

Gloria hummed in thought for a moment. "Tulpas come from human minds. They carry the intelligence from which they are born, among other things."

With that, my shoulders slumped. "Norman's smart."

Gloria snaked an arm around my shoulders. "You are too, Robin. You are your father's son." She gave a gentle squeeze. "And the stone worked. So did your shield, which impresses me because it shows you have mental strength."

"What's going on down here?"

Gloria and I looked towards Dad's sound.

Sweaty from whatever he'd been doing under the house, he appeared a little tired. But his eyes were keen as a blade. One look at me, and his expression turned thoughtful.

"Something happened at the hospital?"

I nodded.

"Is Norman okay?" His eyebrows knitted upon my hesitation. "Maerie." Her name left his lips more like a statement than a question. "What happened?"

I briefly told him the events at the hospital. He listened, nodding at certain points, and remained silent to the end. When I finished, he paused, a thoughtful expression on his face. Then he said, "I read in the paper about two boys found murdered at Central Park. Would they happen to be two others who bullied Norman?"

"Yes," I replied, amazed still at Dad's quick conclusions.

"I said the other day that I think you should stay away

from Norman. This is another warning."

"But Norman's not the--"

Dad held up his hands. "Wait. I didn't say he's the problem... But he's the source of it."

"What do you mean? He's in a bloody coma, Dad!"

Dad's face reflected calm while his voice exuded authority. "Gloria told you the other day about tulpas. You just said you're sure Norman created Maerie... right?"

"Yeah, but --"

"She's killed three boys so far — Louis, Jason, and that other kid — and there will be more."

I shrugged. "Maybe."

"Has it occurred to you that Norman's psyche and memories are feeding Maerie? That she's checking his memories against yours?"

Dad let me process that thought. Then when I opened my mouth to speak, he continued. "Who's next? What about the kids they hung round? How many used to stand around and laugh, or simply laugh, when they bullied him."

I said nothing. Just shrugged.

"And how many will she kill?" He paused to watch my expression, which I tried hard not to change. "And what about the times when you and Norman used to fight and argue about shit? I remember a time the two of you started slapping each other and wrestling because of some crap about which superhero would win a fight in the comic books. Do you remember that?"

Yeah, I did. It had happened three years earlier in seventh grade. Yeah. I was on the Phantom's side of the argument. Norman thought Batman would kick Phantom's butt. I told him Batman was a pansy because he needed a utility belt. Norman thought the Phantom stupid because his lips never moved when he spoke. I said only poofters wore capes. We pushed each other to make our points. Norman gained a blood nose, but the moment he cried at the pain, I stopped, said sorry, and helped clean his face. A bruise shone on his face for the next few days. To protect our friendship, he told his mother he'd run into a pole while playing tiggy. Dad was the only adult who knew the full story.

Dad's voice was firm. "While Norman's in his coma, we have no idea of the extent of his brain damage from hitting his head. Memories could be distorted. If Maerie is reading his memories, she may see you as the bully."

"What?" I shook my head. "No way! I said sorry. We're mates."

"You know that, and so do I. But we don't know what's happened to his memories. He might remember it differently now."

My head throbbed as my frustration grew. The way Dad glared at me said everything and I didn't like it. "You want me to stop being Norman's friend." I knew Dad's unspoken words. "And you don't want me to see Ella anymore."

Dad allowed a small sigh, lowered his gaze for a second, and said, "Whatever it takes. You have to stay safe."

My jaw tensed as I calculated my response. "No."

"Rob--"

"No." My voice set stronger as I allowed the anger to boil in my gut. "I don't turn my back on friends."

"I'm not--"

Anger and determination pushed past my barriers to allow my words to escape. "It doesn't have to be that way, Dad. I'm not letting Norman down just because he's sick or something. I'm going to help him."

I glanced towards Gloria. She was standing to our side, watching on the line between the arguing Mitchells like the umpire at a tennis match. She looked divided as if she didn't know what to say. I respected her silence. Then I glared back at Dad.

"This is my life. I'm not letting go. Not giving up on Norman. Or Ella."

"You have other friends," Dad replied. "You'll find another --"

"Don't even say I'll find another girlfriend either," I snapped. "I don't give up on people I love."

With that, I turned and stomped upstairs, ignoring Dad's words. Gloria spoke to him. Through the corner of my eye, she stopped Dad with a gentle hand. Gentle words.

But nothing soothed me as I stormed to my room and slammed the door shut.

Ten minutes later, Dad and Gloria came back upstairs. Dishes clattered. The sounds of a table set. Soon the aromas of chicken, curry, and rice drifted under my bedroom door and teased my nostrils. My stomach growled. I hadn't eaten for about six hours. But my stubbornness held me steady.

Not even when Dad knocked on my door did I relent to temptation. I ignored it, told him to go away. I was glad Gloria didn't knock. I might have given in.

My taste buds pleaded, but I knew why Dad made the butter chicken. He knew it was my favourite food. I swallowed, pretending my saliva was food. It didn't work. My stomach still growled, hungry like a wolf, and I picked up a Phantom comic to distract myself.

Hushed voices. Dinner-time conversation. The words filtered through my door like ghosts through a wall to my ears. I don't know why I took notice. Maybe someone mentioned my name. So I listened.

"He worries me."

"Yes, but you can't alienate him from those he loves."

"He's too young to love."

"Didn't you at his age?"

"That's different. And I don't like to encourage him with this stuff. Tulpas, shields, and such. He's--"

"His father's son."

A pause.

"Doesn't make it right."

"Neither is it wrong."

"I feel safer knowing he's not with Norman. He's further from Maerie."

"He's smart." A pause. "Anyway, you asked me to help with him. Let me."

The voices faded. I stepped back from the wall, shocked.

Gloria wasn't here just because she was Dad's girlfriend. She was here because he wanted help with me?

Suddenly, everything seemed unfair and fake. What I thought was different. I couldn't trust Dad, nor Gloria, which was a shame because I liked her. What she had taught me about the shielding worked, even if I needed more practice.

But I couldn't stay here. I needed space, to think, to be alone.

Where could I go?

# CHAPTER 26

Her voice through the door was fearsome. "Yes? Who is it?"

I cleared my throat. "Aunty Deb. It's me. Robin."

Softer now. "Rob?"

Three chains slid from their latches and the lock clicked before the heavy front door opened. Dressed in her t-shirt and a pair of shorts, she stood there, surprise painted on her face. "What are you doing here?" She looked past me onto the front porch. "Is it just you?"

I nodded. "I didn't tell Dad I'm here."

"It's 10pm. Why are you out so late?" She remained in the doorway.

"I had to, Aunty Deb. Sorry. I couldn't stay at home."

Curiosity replaced her surprise as Aunty Deb let me enter. "What's happened?"

"Thanks." I stepped through the front door, carrying my canvas backpack filled with two t-shirts and underwear. "I needed to get away."

Aunty Deb led me through the hallway past the living room, where Matlock showed on the television, to the kitchen. Her home, more modern than Dad's house, was inviting to me. The glass table looked pristine, futuristic by comparison to the wooden table at home. It reminded me of a hotel unit.

She showed me the chair. "Sit there. I'll call your Dad and --"

"No, don't," I said. "He doesn't know--"

"Robin Mitchell!" She afforded me a stern look over her glasses. "That's why I am calling him. If he's found you're missing, it will worry him." Her tone softened. "You know how he gets when he's worried."

No, I didn't. I never saw him like that, apart from the

other day when he wore his sunglasses inside the house.

My aunt took her cordless phone, a recent phenomenon in Middleville, and pressed a button. "It's ringing. Have some biscuits," she said, bobbing her head at a pack of Tim Tams with one biscuit missing from its plastic tray. Her tone changed when the call connected. "Hello? Bill? It's Deb." She paused. "I'm well, thanks. Yes, it's late. Sorry about that. Your son is here." After a glance in my direction, "Yes, Robin. How many other sons do you have?" Her eyes rolled in her sockets.

Meanwhile, I took a Tim Tam and devoured it quicker than a Hoover before I realised it. A grumble escaped my belly, so I allowed myself one more. Although Aunty Deb wanted me to help myself, I didn't want to make a guts of myself. So I ate the next biscuit slower to savour the sweet chocolatey treat.

Before long, Aunty Deb finished the phone call, hanging the receiver on its wall cradle, and regarded me with a pondering expression. I stopped chewing to return her gaze. She said nothing; the silence unnerved me.

"Dad's coming for me, isn't he?"

"No. You can stay here." Her face was serious as she sat opposite me at the dining table, but she softened before speaking more. "Your Dad didn't say much and assumes I don't know he's hiding something. What's going on, Robbie?"

I collected my thoughts, my eyes resting on the Tim Tams. Aunty Deb caught my gaze.

"Your father said you didn't eat dinner. Would you like a sandwich?" My stomach growled in response which elicited an amused smile from Aunty Deb. "Come on. I'll get one for you."

Aunty Deb retrieved the ingredients for a ham and cheese sandwich from the fridge, slapping it together, while I told her the story. I started with Louis' death, telling her about the dream I had the night before the police came. When I reached the bit about the nightmare of the shark biting my face, and how I woke bleeding, her actions slowed in surprise.

Aunty Deb sat in shock and disbelief. She surveyed my face. "You have no scars. Are you telling stories?" I shook my head. "No," she agreed, "it's not your style." Standing, she grabbed my plate and rinsed it under the tap. There she lingered, palms on the sink's edge, as she processed everything.

"It's all true, Aunty Deb," I said to break the uncomfortable silence. "I'm not crazy or lying."

Aunty Deb said nothing. Wheels turned in her head with the same facial expression as Dad when he mulled over things. "Tell me more about your father's girlfriend. What's her name?"

"Oh, yeah. Her name's Gloria. She--"

Aunty Deb's mouth gaped open and her eyes widened.

"What?" I said. "What is it?"

"Gloria, you say?"

I nodded. "Yeah. Why?"

"Describe her."

I complied, describing everything but her nakedness at the first meeting. Aunt Deb's eyes opened wider in surprise.

"What's up?" I asked.

"Robin, what's the strangest thing you noticed about Gloria?"

I shrugged. "She is great at reading hands."

Aunty Deb hesitated, looking upward to the corner of her eye, and shook her head. "Have you noticed something about her looks?"

Curious about my aunt's interest in Gloria's looks, I opened my mouth to question. She remained silent, waiting for my reply.

"She looks like Mum did, I guess." As the words left my mouth, a wordless notion crept across my mind.

"Your mother's name was Elizabeth Jenkins." Aunty Deb sat as she said the words, her eyes reflecting her recollection of memories. "But she preferred her middle name: Gloria."

Surprise purged my mind of coherent words. "What?" Nothing else escaped, at least, nothing I understood. "Are you saying?"

Aunty Deb gazed at me a moment, her expression thoughtful. "Yes. That was her name. And you say she learned Buddhism?"

Slowly I nodded. "Yeah. You're not saying Gloria is my mother?"

Aunty Deb laughed. "No. What made you think so? Her name?"

"Her resemblance to Mum," I admitted. "I just never connected the dots."

"It's funny how your Dad found someone like your mother. Same name, the same looks." Aunty Deb laughed, patted my shoulder, then her eyes darkened a moment later. "I'm concerned about the rest you told me though. Normally, I wouldn't presume it. If not for what your father said..."

"What did Dad say?"

"Nothing out of the ordinary." She removed her glasses and rubbed her eyes. "It's what he didn't say that makes me wonder."

"Do you believe me?"

Aunty Deb rose and approached the table upon which the television stood. After switching the television off, she withdrew a photo album from the shelf beside it and flicked through it. "Ah! Here it is." She held it for me to see. "You reminded me of this."

I took the heavy album and peered where her finger rested. A picture of my father as a younger man. Beside him stood a shorter young woman with a smile I hadn't seen since I was a little boy. It was Mum holding a baby in her arms. Me.

Then something else struck me. Her expression was the same as another I'd seen recently. I blinked and peered closer.

It could have been Gloria. The Gloria I knew looked like my mother did when I was a baby. Did she remind him of his wife; my mother?

No, it couldn't be.

I glanced at my Aunty Deb who was watching me with intent curiosity. Her eyebrows arched a little. "Well?"

I looked back at the photo again. Another thunderbolt arced through my memory.

Flags. Coloured flags. I'd experienced the memory recently and not recognised it. For there behind us stood a large Tibetan-styled temple. The same I had seen flash through my mind when Maerie had probed earlier through my memories.

It was a real memory. Maerie had seen it, but what use did she find in it?

# CHAPTER 27

Once I learned a legend. If we dream of someone, they are thinking of us. But that night, I dreamed of the events before my sister had died.

A five-year-old whirlwind of terror and fun, Anne-maree loved stirring trouble for me. On that last day, moreso.

Norman and I were playing cricket with a tennis ball in the backyard. Mum had said to let Anne-maree play, too, which I hated. Who wants their bratty little sister playing with him and his best friend? So uncool. Although mad about the idea, I held it in.

Anne-maree had lined up a bunch of her dolls and stuffed toys like spectators to watch the game.

"Come on," Norman called to Anne-maree. "Head over there to catch out Robin now he's batting."

But she messed around, talking to her Snoopy doll with a sing-song voice. "Does little Snoopy want to play too?"

Norman's eyes rolled in their sockets as my sister placed Snoopy where she should have stood. "Anne-maree!"

But my little sister only giggled and toddled to sit with the other toys and chat with them.

"Come on, Norman," I called. "Just bowl, will you?"

Even then, Norman was a long-limbed kid. He circled at the other end of the yard, took a run-up, and bowled the ball towards me. I tapped it, and the ball sailed Snoopy who proved incapable of catching. The ball's momentum sent the stuffed doll rolling along the ground like a skittle. Anne-maree screamed and ran out towards the dog and cuddled him close.

"That's unfair," she whined. "Snoopy wasn't ready, and you hit the ball too hard for him, Robin! You hurt him."

I laughed and kept running while Norman ran for the ball

and threw it at the wicket and missed. "Snoopy needs to learn to play better, doesn't he?"

Don't laugh at your little sister if she's playing with your Steve Austin doll. She ran with her Snoopy doll towards the other toys, and I realised too late. She picked up the bionic man. One hand grasped his body, and the other his head. I reached her just as she snapped Steve's head off his shoulders with a crack.

Angry, I pushed Anne-maree so hard she tumbled to the grass with a thud, and she cried. Her lower lip trembling, she ran behind the brick incinerator, her sobs loud enough to evoke a sick feeling in my stomach.

"Why didja push her so hard?" Norman scowled at me as he ran to her. "She's your little sister."

At that moment, Mum appeared on the back stairs. "Robin, what's going on? Why is Anne-maree crying?"

"He pushed me over, Mummy!" Anne-maree barrelled into my mother's waiting arms, giving me a dirty look before pouring on more sobs. The crying was faked. I knew because I hadn't pushed so hard as Norman said. Cunning as a shithouse rat, my sister was an expert in emotional manipulation and could turn things to her favour. Even if...

"She broke my Steve Austin doll," I complained.

I still remember the way my mother's hair shone in the sun so she looked like an angel with a halo. She appraised the situation, looked at the bionic man's headless corpse, noted Anne-maree's skinned elbow from her fall, and made us stand to face each other. "Both of you apologise to each other."

But we didn't. We eyed each other like warring cats ready to strike.

"Go on," Mum said. "Say sorry."

The long seconds hung and stretched as we faced each other. Anne-maree's dark stormy eyes of molten chocolate glared at me. I stared back at her. Mum cleared her throat.

"Well?"

The anger boiled my belly. No way did I want to

apologise. But Mum was insistent. The question was who would say sorry first.

"Be a gentleman," Norman hissed to me. "You hafta say it first."

I stood still as a statue, defiant.

"Go on," my friend urged. I wanted to deck Norman then, but it wasn't worth the trouble.

"I'm sorry," I started, "but you shouldn't have broken Steve Austin."

There! That felt good to say it.

"M-uuuuuuuuuuum!"

Mum's voice was insistent and firm. "Anne-maree, say sorry too. You don't break your brother's toys either."

Seeming ages later, Anne-maree looked down at the ground. "I'm sorry too, because you hit Snoopy with the tennis ball and you shouldn't have done that."

"What?" I fumed, ready to belt my sister for real.

"Hey, look!" Norman called from the side, holding up Steve in his hands. "I fixed his head!"

"See?" Mum said. "That's much better. Anne-maree, clean up and come along. We're going out to the shops soon." Then my mother, Angel of the Stars, turned and headed under the house towards the laundry.

Anne-maree waited, stalked over and snatched Steve Austin from my hands. In a flash, she reefed off his head and bionic arm, before she twisted his legs in opposite directions and punched his crotch. "I'm sorry I didn't hurt him."

Then she tossed Steve's twisted body to the ground and walked inside with her toys as I picked up the pieces.

"She's a farty cow," I muttered, examining Steve and putting his limbs back on with Norman's help. "A stinky poo farty cow."

But why did Norman watch after Anne-maree with such a smile? "Yeah," he sighed, the hint of a smile on his face. "She is."

Inside, I silently wished Anne-maree would die. Worse, that wish came true. Worse still, Mum died in the same car accident. And I couldn't take it back.

The dream repeated itself. Must have been two or three times. And each time, the growing dread inside me increased more than earlier.

It was late in the evening. Bathed and dressed in my Star Wars pyjamas, I watched The Bionic Woman, for whom I held a boyhood crush. Dad was acting strangely, agitated more when I asked when Mum and Anne-maree would be back. Not long after, the phone rang. Dad answered it, and his voice changed, deepened and seemed to slur. Before long, he rang Aunty Deb, his voice hushed and low as he spoke. It was a short call. Aunty Deb arrived just as The Bionic Woman finished. Dad left soon after, his keys jingling as he headed out the door. Somehow Aunty Deb entertained me until Dad arrived home a couple hours later. I was in bed, but I heard him come home. By that time, I missed Mum heaps, and I saw the kitchen light shining on Dad's darkened tear-soaked face. His strong hands woke me and picked me up to hug me close, his body shuddering with each mournful sob. And I cried.

After the third or fourth time I relived the dream of my memory, I at last woke. A skeletal finger of silvery light from the outside street light poked through the window and rested upon the foot of my bed.

The hand was gentle as it touched my skin, but its graveyard frigidity startled me to full wakefulness as my eyes opened wider. There beside me stood my little sister, her skin translucent. At my surprise, she lifted a little finger to her mouth and winked. Before my disbelieving eyes she grew tall and slender as she would have been had she lived longer.

A moment later she faded in the growing dawn to disappear from sight as I lapsed into shocked unconsciousness.

And I knew.

# CHAPTER 28

Later that morning, Dad arrived to take me home, which was a shame. I wanted to ride home alone.

Dad said little and spoke only when needed. His face betrayed little of his thoughts, yet I understood he restrained something. When he loaded my bike, I imagined him holding back anger as he shoved the frame in the Landcruiser.

"Get in," he said finally, reaching into his pocket for his keys.

"Bill," Aunty Deb called from the front door, dressed in her business clothes. "Can I have a word?"

"We have to go," he replied without altering his direction.

"You're on holiday, Bill." Her voice had the same firm tone she used on Detective Crane. "You have time."

Dad sighed and walked back to his younger sister while I waited by the passenger's door. When he reached her, she said a few things to him, her eyes glancing once or twice at me. For me, they offered a small smile, whereas they appeared sterner on him. He glanced at me and turned back to her with a nod before returning to the vehicle. Aunty Deb called me over, too, and hugged me tight.

"Thanks for visiting me, Robin. Never mind your Dad." She ruffled my hair and grinned. "And don't forget the photo, okay?"

I nodded. After the night's strange dreams, I'd forgotten it.

She winked. "Go on. He's waiting."

On the way home, Dad asked if I wanted to go fishing. I shrugged although I knew he wanted to talk. His idea of chilling or talking always meant fishing. I wanted to talk, just didn't want to do it while hanging my rod over the water. Maybe my dreams and recent experiences did that. Who knew what its muddy waters hid? So I said nothing. Just looked out the window at the houses we passed, not taking notice.

When we reached home, Dad stepped out of the Landcruiser, saying, "I'll be on the back verandah. I'd love it if you joined me too." He offered me a gentle smile, not too enthusiastic, but enough to be sincere. The real Dad.

I only nodded as I took my bike from the back of the Landcruiser and wheeled it under the house. Heaps of things passed through my head. The photo Aunty Deb showed me of Dad with Mum, who looked just like a slightly younger version of Gloria. A rainbow of Tibetan prayer flags that flapped in the breeze behind us in the picture. The dream of Anne-maree and the apparition at the foot of my bed. My mind gnawed over the details, knowing everything happened for a reason and connected them, but for what purpose?

I had to talk to Dad. So after dumping my backpack in my room, I headed to the back verandah.

My father was sitting in his favourite chair, regarding the poinciana tree's leaves as they blew lazily in the breeze. A cup of coffee in his hand, from which he took a sip. He waited a few heartbeats before turning his gaze towards me as I sat in a chair on the opposite side of a small table between us.

My mind burned with questions. Purpose filled me, determined to find answers.

Dad's voice was even and calm. "A lot's happened in the past couple of weeks, hasn't it?" I nodded and opened my mouth to speak, but he beat me to it. "Let me explain some things." He sipped more coffee. "Things about your mother, Gloria, and about what's going on with Norman."

I remained quiet as Dad answered the questions I meant to ask. How did he do that?

"I guess your Aunty Deb showed you an old photo of us. You, me, and your mother." His grey eyes watched mine, waiting for an answer.

I nodded. "Yeah. Mum looks like Gloria."

He took a sip and swallowed. "Yes, she does."

"The photo was taken in Tibet, wasn't it?"

"Nepal, actually. Your mother and I travelled there and to Tibet before we conceived you. That's how we met."

"I was born there?" That was news to me. I always thought, or assumed, I'd been born in Middleville at the Mater, or even the Base hospital.

He nodded.

"How?"

"How were you born?"

I shook my head. "No, I mean, how did you meet overseas? Didn't you both come from Middleville?"

He smiled, lazed back in his chair, and looked up at the ceiling. "I was born here, went to the school on Main Street and attended high school. After I finished, I took a few jobs on fishing boats. One job took me to Singapore. There I met a Buddhist chap. We hit it off as mates, and I soon travelled to India, then Tibet and Nepal. I loved it so much I stayed."

"What about Mum?"

"We met at the same monastery with the thought-dragon Gloria told you about."

Astonishment opened my mouth. "No way! You were there?"

He nodded. "I was known there as Jungney. That's where I met your mother. One thing led to another, you were born, and we returned to Australia."

"Jungney?" I asked. The name sounded familiar.

"The monk who created the thought-form."

Surprise cranked my brain into overdrive. "The tulpa? You created the dragon tulpa?"

"Yes."

The answer slid into my brain like a tumbler in a lock. "No way!"

Dad allowed a fleeting smile. "Yeah way. I'd been studying a long time, came across some scrolls in the library, some forbidden to my eyes. Like any good student..." He gave a slow shrug.

Heat rose from my belly. "Why didn't you tell me before?"

"You might not have believed me, and I thought it best to tell you to leave Norman alone." He paused and sipped from his coffee, looking over the cup's edge at me.

Questions, lots of them, flew through my head like pieces of paper in a whirlwind. Which should I choose?

"What happened to the tulpa you created?"

"It flew away, found another dragon, and had babies with it. They grew up and ate everyone up." He laughed upon seeing my gullible look change to rolling eyes. At last, he sobered. "Seriously, I had to reabsorb the dragon."

"Reabsorb?"

"It came from my mind. My thoughts gave it life. I had to take it back."

"Why?"

"In time, the dragon started to change. At first, it was a furry little ball of delight. Then it grew cheeky. Adventurous. Later, it changed further on its own, became difficult to control, so I took it back before irreversible damage happened."

"Sort of like Norman and Maerie?"

"Mm-hmm."

I considered this a moment. "He's in a coma. How can he do it?"

Dad closed his eyes. "I don't know."

"How did you know Maerie was a tulpa?" I asked. "Was it at the hospital?"

He shook his head. "Before that. On your last fortnight before holidays, Norman stopped by in the morning. That's when I first saw Maerie beside him. I nearly asked who she was. Then I realised she cast no shadow."

"And you said nothing?"

Dad shook his head. "I didn't know for sure. Sometimes ghosts appear the same way."

"Ghosts?" I looked at him in surprise. "You don't believe in ghosts."

"The truth is I'm not afraid of no ghost." He winked when I caught the reference. "But I acknowledge their existence. I just don't yet know if it's the deceased person's consciousness or a thought projection - as opposed to a tulpa."

I remembered my dream. "I saw Anne-maree this morning, I think."

Dad's eyes rose. "Oh?"

"I dreamed of the last day I saw her, of how Norman and I were playing with her. She broke my Steve Austin doll, so I wished her dead."

A sad expression fell over Dad's face. He leaned across from his chair, stretched a hand out to me, and squeezed my arm. "You didn't kill them, kid. Some dumb-arse truck driver was up to his eyeballs with uppers lost control of his truck. That's how Anne-maree died. It wasn't you."

"But her ghost stood at the foot of the bed."

Dad paused, wheels turned behind his eyes, and he shook his head. "Part of your dream."

"Dad," I said. "If you could create a tulpa back then, and Norman did too..." The question caught in my throat. It seemed too crazy to ask.

"What?"

"Gloria looks like Mum. Even sounds the way I remember she did. Is she-"

Dad hesitated. A strange expression on his face, he turned away from me and looked across the back yard. "You assume I created a tulpa of your mother."

# CHAPTER 29

"Do you realise how sick that sounds?" Dad asked, a belly laugh escaping.

"But I saw you looking at the picture of Mum and Annemaree the other day," I replied. "Remember, after my face bled?"

Dad stopped laughing, but his body still shook as he suppressed it. "Yeah, but I don't miss your mother enough to bring her back from the dead."

The words sounded terrible as they left his lips. My mouth opened in shock, the words stuck. At last, my father quit laughing and the serious tone returned.

"I need not bring her back to life, nor to create a tulpa of her. If I did, I would restore your sister too."

Memory came of hearing Dad's bedhead thumping against the wall and Gloria's giggles from his room the other night. It seemed sick to suppose he was rooting something from his head. What would you call that? Mind-fucking? The idea made me laugh too. Another realisation dawned upon me. Norman had created a tulpa for the same reason. Did he get his jollies with Maerie?

"Sorry, Dad. With recent events, I..."

"No worries." Dad wiped away a mirthful tear of laughter. "It reminds me of something."

# CHAPTER 30

A knock at the front door interrupted Dad. I wanted to ignore the door and ask Dad what he meant.

"Go see who's there," he said. "Probably a God-botherer or salesman. Tell them we're not interested."

No God-botherers stood at the door. Only Ella who proved a sight for sore eyes, her smile shining upon seeing me. I smiled in return through the front glass louvres as I rounded the corner to the front door. As I opened the door, I spied someone else with her.

John O'Sullivan!

My heart tripped and stumbled as his eyes returned my gaze.

"Hi." Ella stepped inside and briefly hugged me. So relaxed and confident despite her ex's presence. I merely nodded towards John.

"What's he doing here?"

John offered an easy smile which was so characteristic of him. I always found John easy to get along with, even if he hung with Stubbs and Crane and the others. On his own, I liked John. But why was he with his ex? At my place? "I dropped by at Ella's this morning to pick up something of mine that Norman had." He lifted a D&D adventure book. "I lent it to him months ago. Ella suggested I tag along here."

He moved to come inside and stopped when I refused to move.

Ella's gentle hand rested upon mine. "Please, let him in. I asked him here." My brow creased, and Ella gave me a reassuring smile. "It's okay. It's about Norman."

John faced Ella. "Have you told him?"

Ella shook her head, and the way she looked at John, my heart hit a lump of coral and started to sink.

John recognised my expression. "It's not like that,

Robbo." His straight white teeth flashed in the morning's sunlight. He paused and added with a slight lisp. "May I say you're looking good this morning?" When I turned to glare at him, he laughed. "It's okay. Ella's with you, mate. I'm not interested in Ella." His words hung a moment longer. "Or any other girl."

From nowhere, the invisible penny plummeted to the ground and rang. My jaw dropped. "You mean you're a -"

He nodded, and a hint of nervousness tinged his words. "Can you keep it down low? Ella's the only one who knows. I haven't even told my other friends."

I moved aside to allow him inside. "Do you mean like the ones who died at Central Park?"

His eyeballs rolled. "No! Especially not them. And they weren't gay either." He offered me his hand, which I hesitated in taking. Talk in the 1980s of AIDS and how it started with "poofters" was big in Middleville. Few people in Middleville tolerated gay men. I have to admit, with the lack of exact information, I was one of their haters. But I never bashed them.

John was about to let his hand drop when I swallowed my fear and shook it. Yet a part of me accepted his hand because I was glad he wasn't interested in Ella more than to accept him as a genuine guy.

"Come on in," I said, staying pleasant for Ella's sake.

"You're right about his hair," John said to Ella, with a sideways wink to me.

"Stop teasing him," Ella replied to him. "You can be such a bitch. And stop checking out my boyfriend's arse."

John lifted his hands in mock shock and denial and grinned with Ella. We laughed; I laughed a little less, but it felt good. Then Ella lifted her backpack for me to see.

"Are you running away from home too?" I asked.

"What?"

"Never mind," I said. "Come on out the back."

"Is your Dad home?"

"Yeah," I answered, leading the way, and called ahead.

"Hey, Dad! We have company."

My father who had been gazing across the back yard again looked up and greeted Ella as she entered. A curious look crossed his face as he saw John, who Ella introduced. He shook John's hand in greeting, and said, "It's good to see you following your true self."

Taken aback, John blinked back. Dad smiled. "It's not always healthy to hide yourself."

I did a double-take. So did John. "You knew?"

Dad only offered an enigmatic smile. "Would you both," he glanced at Ella and John, "like something to drink?"

They both said coffee sounded good and Dad moved out to the kitchen. Once we were alone, John whispered, "How did your Dad know that I --"

I shrugged. "No idea, John. Ask him that."

"Anyway," Ella interrupted, "we have news for you on the Maerie story." She reached into her canvas knapsack and pulled out a notebook.

I regarded the battered thick volume with a questioning eye as Ella thrust it towards me. Taking it, I opened its pages. Norman's handwriting covered each page. Norman never stayed with one form of writing. Sometimes, he would write sentences in cursive writing, then he'd swap to block writing, before returning to the former. Our English teachers always complained when he presented essays for assessment.

"This is Norman's diary," I said in surprise. "You found it."

"Under his mattress," Ella confirmed. "He kept it under one side of the mattress, but he moved it after I found it last time. I had to lift his whole mattress to get it from the centre of the bed."

"Paranoid much about you?" John interjected and raised his hands in mock horror when Ella delivered an evil stare at him.

"I bookmarked parts for you."

It felt wrong to view my friend's private thoughts, yet a surge of voyeuristic excitement oozed over me as I flicked towards the pieces of forbidden knowledge marked by Ella's yellow bookmark. The words glared at me from an entry dated a few months earlier.

སྦལ་པ་

*Can't get that song out of my head. Glory of Love. It's been a whole damn week since I saw the movie. And the song lingers in my head. I enjoyed the movie. There's just one problem. It reminds me of how single I am.*

*Having no girlfriend makes me feel like a loser. Worse still I can't bring myself to talk to any girl I want. Robin doesn't have any trouble. He's single, too, but I'm sure he could get one easily. I could almost see him with Ella. That'd be radical. My best mate as a brother-in-law. But Ella seems to like the jock types more. The ones who would treat her like a steaming pile of cow turd.*

*So, Diary, I guess I'm whingeing tonight about not having a girlfriend, being lonely as all fuck, and having a pity party about it.*

*But I have another idea. These books I found in the library. All I wanted was to learn about astral travelling, what it would be like to leave my body at night and travel to other places. I guess I'd first visit a supermodel's shower while she's in it. What if she could see me? I'd probably scare the shit out of her.*

*No, I found something better. One of these books takes a weird tangent and talks about thought projection. Next it describes the ability to create life from a thought. Something like that Buddhist saying on Monkey Magic: With our thoughts, we create the world.*

*I don't want to create worlds. I just want a girlfriend, a dream lover, a girl who loves me, would do anything for me, would let me love her without laughing at me like I'm some freak. Is that too much to ask?*

*But there's only one girl I remember loving. That was so long ago. She never laughed at me. Yes, she was a bitch in her little girl way. That was Robin's sister, Anne-maree, but she's dead. I can't bring her back, but what if I could create a new version of her just by thinking and meditating on her like this book says?*

*I'm glad I have this Polaroid photo of her, taken days before she died. It helps me remember how she looked.*

*Another funny thing. In this D&D book I borrowed from John O'Sullivan, Drums on Fire Mountain. It has a non-player character in it called Maerie. She has the same expression in her eyes as Anne-maree. It's almost like the artist knew Anne-maree and drew an older version of her, the way she would be. She's beautiful as she grows older. I could kiss her. And even cooler. It reminds me how Anne-maree, being a little kid then, couldn't speak her full name. She always called herself Maree, but she pronounced it as "May Ree". So cute. Yes, I'll try to replicate what those Canadian students did in 1972. I'll create a whole history of Anne-maree, let her call herself Maerie, and bring her to life. Just like they did with the Philip Experiments.*

*A part of it scares me. But I can improve upon their mistakes. I can make her the nicest person for me.*

*I will.*

སྦྲལ་བ་

Dad returned from the kitchen while I read that part of Norman's journal. He didn't know what I read, but he recognised the worry in my eyes that something wasn't right.

"Norman based his tulpa on Anne-maree."

Dad's sunburned skin paled at his deceased daughter's name. Quickly handing the steaming coffees to Ella and John, he took the journal. His lips moved in silent whispers as his eyes darted across the pages, flicking through and taking in the story. Then he showed me some pages ahead, filled with drawings, and yes, some looked like Anne-maree as an older girl. Character sketches and descriptions on each page.

"That's almost the rest of the book," Ella said, sipping her coffee. "He was like totally obsessed on her. There's an entry there too, around about October, where she finally appeared to him. It was at the library. She talked to him through thoughts at first until she was strong enough to speak with her voice."

Dad's sombre eyes regarded me as he closed Norman's journal. "Thanks, Ella." He handed it to her with a faint smile. "I was telling Robin that I saw the tulpa with Norman in the last weeks of your exams before the term finished. I recognised what she was, and then I met her in the hospital."

Ella's face dropped. "You knew? How?"

"Dad created one in Tibet. He was the monk that Gloria told me about."

Ella's eyes lost focus as she stroked her chin. "What happened to the dragon you created, Mr Mitchell?"

"I had to reabsorb it."

"What do you mean?" John asked. "How would you reabsorb it?"

"A tulpa is a creature of intense thought permeating reality. It becomes one with our universe." Dad paused for a moment and shrugged. "I just took it back to me."

"Can you reabsorb Maerie the same way?"

My father shook his head. "No. Norman created it. Only he can do it, and..." He shrugged again.

"Can we kill her?" I asked. "She's not a real person."

"Kill?" Dad's eyebrows raised. "How do you kill an idea that has become flesh?"

"Perhaps if we created another tulpa to tackle her?"

A smile crossed Dad's face, and he shook his head in a hopeless attitude. "It took me months to create the one I made. I meditated day and night. For some time, I even stopped eating and drinking just to meditate on my own."

"Norman never starved himself." Ella leaned forward and rested her chin on her knuckles.

"But he took a long time to create it," Dad replied. "He also showed great passion, determination, and a belief in himself to create it. Look at the detail in which he drew

Maerie." We looked at each other while he explained his thoughts. "But that's not all," he said. "The three of you could create something, perhaps even with my help, but there's something else."

"What? I asked.

"You're running out of time."

"Time?"

Dad reached over to the tiny table beside his chair and retrieved the newspaper to show its headlines.

TEEN CRITICALLY INJURED IN FREAK ACCIDENT

Stunned, I glanced at both Ella and John to see their expressions. Did they know about this? The surprise on their faces confirmed I wasn't alone.

Dad's quiet voice explained what I read.

"It's Richard Crane. The son of the detective who questioned you at the station." He took a breath. "A ceiling fan fell on him while he slept."

I handed back the newspaper to him. "Chopped him. He's in hospital."

"Which one?" John asked.

"The Mater," Dad told him. "That's where Norman is. I doubt that she made a mistake by not killing him outright. How much did Richard bully Norman?"

"Nothing much," Ella replied. "Might have dacked him a few times."

But John shook his head. "No, Richard did more than that." He turned towards me. "Around about the time you were in hospital having your appendix removed, back in primary school days, he caught Norman in the school yard."

"How?"

"The kids from sixth and seventh grade used to play Red Rover. Remember?" He waited for me to nod. "Well, Norman was in the middle. Richard was one those running from one end to the other. Well, Norman went to tag Richard, but Richard ran straight for him. I thought at the time he was bluffing Norman into running away so he could pass without being tagged. Norman tried to avoid him, and Richard ploughed right through him. Knocked Norman to the ground and hurt Norman's arm. Remember?"

A vague recollection surfaced. Norman had his arm in a cast at one point. He visited me in hospital with it, and I signed the plaster with a dirty limerick about Tarzan.

"I'd forgotten that."

"Norman has a long memory," Dad said. "I'd say he didn't forgive Richard for it, if that's all Richard did."

"There were other times, too," John admitted. "Like flushing his head down the toilet in ninth grade... without making sure it was empty first."

"And where were you?" I challenged John. "Were you and Matthew Stubbs holding him in?"

A guilty expression crossed Ella's ex-boyfriend's face as he gave a slow nod. "Yeah, I did. And that's when I realised I was wrong. Something changed my perspective. I apologised to Norman soon afterwards, about when I started going out with Ella."

I couldn't hold back my thoughts towards John. "You did it to save your skin."

Dad's hand on my arm distracted me.

"Cool your jets, Robin." He nodded to John. "What happened after that? Did Norman forgive you?"

"Yeah." He held up the D&D book. "I used to loan him books from my Dungeons and Dragons. That's how we bonded. And to make things more solid, I told the others to leave Norman too. They were still jerks though." Then he looked at me. "And Robin, maybe you're right about me saving my skin. But I made up for it. Maybe I realised they could have bullied me if they knew I was gay."

That silenced me, made me think.

And I realised Dad's thinking eyes were on too. "Who else remains?"

"Just Matthew Stubbs."

Dad shook his head. "Then there's just you three remaining."

"What?" My jaw dropped quicker than a skank's panties. "Why us?"

"While Norman's in a coma, Maerie is on a rampage. She's dealing with the bullies who hurt the love of her life, her creator. And she's showing no remorse. When she's done, there are those who pose a danger to her: you, Ella, and John."

"Us?" Ella's voice cracked. "Why?"

"Because you know the truth about her. You can damage her existence which would keep her away from Norman, the boy she fiercely defends."

"If you can't create a tulpa to fight her in time, and we can't create one," I said, "then we're stuffed."

Dad chuckled. "I didn't say there's nothing we can do."

# CHAPTER 31

Dad had a simple plan: avoid Norman and Maerie. But simple doesn't mean easy. For as practical as Dad's initial thoughts appeared, challenges presented themselves. Especially for Ella.

"He's my brother," she said. "How am I not going to visit him in hospital?"

"She's right," John told us. "Mrs Cole's a control freak. Hitler's a wimp by comparison."

Dad snorted with an amused expression, but his eyes kept their thoughtful light. For a moment, he regarded Ella as the wheels turned in his head. "What about your father?"

Ella's brow arched in curiosity. "My Dad? What about him?"

"Would he support your decision? The other night before we went skating, he said he had caught something strange about Maerie too."

Surprised, Ella didn't blink for half a minute. "Really?" Relief filled her features as tension left her features. "I didn't know that."

I nodded. "He said Maerie has no shadow. If you spoke with him, perhaps he might support your decision."

"He doesn't visit Norman as much as Mum does," Ella said. "I figured it was because he worked and didn't have much time."

Dad said nothing. Just let everything sink in for Ella so she could process everything.

"And they've been fighting about it too. Mum reckons Dad never truly connected with Norman and that he uses work as an excuse. But I don't believe it."

The rest of us watched until she finally decided. "Okay. I'll see Dad at work."

Then I looked at Dad. "But is avoiding Norman enough?

What's to stop Maerie coming to us like she did the others?"

A mental image of Richard Crane's injuries from a dropped ceiling fan flashed in front of me, and I shuddered.

"How did the onyx go for you?" Dad asked.

"Maerie used my mother to cut it off me," Ella replied. "That's how she forced Robin to drop his mental shield."

Dad nodded, a thoughtful expression tinged with sadness on his face. "She's a smart bitch. Norman modelled her too much like my little girl." He paused. A slight twitch appeared at his lip. "But she's not Anne-maree." Then he rose from his chair, excused himself before stalking inside, and soon reappeared with a small wooden box with a Tibetan scene carved in its exterior. "Pieces from my days in Nepal," he explained as he opened it and extracted more black stones for all of us. He placed one on himself.

"Ella," he said, "you are welcome to stay here for a while if things are difficult at home." Then he regarded her and me with a sly look. "Don't get any ideas though." With a look at John, he added, "You can stay too."

John laughed. "Okay. And don't worry. I won't get any ideas about Robin."

"What are we going to do?" I repeated. "For how long do we hide?"

"We're not hiding. We're training."

Dad gave me and Ella a lift into town so she could speak to her father. We parked on the riverbank below Victoria Parade and walked with Ella towards the bank where Mr Cole worked on the river's end of Ryan Street. There on the outside footpath we waited. It must have been about ten-or-fifteen minutes before Ella emerged with her father in tow.

His face appeared more worn than the last time. Yet he managed a smile for me and warmly shook my hand then my father's.

"Ella and I chatted," he commented to my father. "I take it you know Ruth is ... peculiar of late."

My father nodded. "I suspected as much." The way he said it, I wondered if he meant because of Norman's condition or because of Maerie's influence. "Have you noticed anything else?"

"Do you mean that Maerie girl?" He looked at us, then at Ella. "Yes. I told Robin my thoughts on her." Mr Cole watched me as he spoke. I held his gaze, and after a thoughtful moment, he bobbed his head in confirmation. "I trust you. Ella has told me a bit about you, and Norman said you're a good man. Is Ella safe with you, Bill?"

"Yes." Dad kept his gaze even upon Mr Cole. "But I'm concerned for you too. This must create a strain."

Ella had told us her father was sleeping in a spare room of late.

Mr Cole's eyes studied me for a few seconds before he answered. "We'll manage. I'll deal with Ruth. I'm unsure what I'll tell her yet, but don't worry. She can be funny about girls and boys together."

Dad retrieved another black onyx from his pocket and handed it to Mr Cole. "You may need this. Keep it on you at all times."

A puzzled expression crossed Mr Cole's face as he took the polished stone and rolled it in his hand. "Onyx! What the-?" Then he realised. "Ah! I saw something similar in India." He pocketed it. "Yes, I understand. Thank you." He hesitated, pondering, his brow set. "Bill, my children - Norman and Ella..."

Dad's expression was solemn when he answered. "Yes."

They shook hands. Mr Cole hugged his daughter hard before he disappeared through the bank's front door.

Dad remained still for a moment, regarded Ella as she fidgeted with her top button. "If your mother's not home, we can stop by your place for whatever you can fit in an overnight bag."

And so, the end began.

# CHAPTER 32

The following seven days proved brutal for us. We stayed in the house for almost the entire time. Dad, me, Ella and John. I camped in the lounge as Ella bunked in my room. John slept in the spare room. Only Dad had his own bed, and Gloria came to stay too.

The two of them acted as our teachers, but only after Dad and Gloria had performed their own ritual upon the house: a cleansing. Pure tones resonated from a Tibetan singing bowl, made of brass, a souvenir Dad kept from his old days at the temple. The ringing penetrated my centre as he rubbed the wooden mallet round its circumference much the same as when you make a glass sing by running a wet finger along its rim.

Meanwhile, Gloria checked each room of the house. In each room, she placed a single black stone each corner of the house and the property. All the while, Dad continued playing the singing bowl. By the end of the ritual, John looked ready to scream as he rolled his eyes. "What the hell is that noise supposed to do?" he asked, wrapping a pillow round his ears. When I told him what Dad said — that it cleanses the environment and wards off evil — John scoffed with a crafty and sarcastic grin. "It nearly made me leave. What's that say about me?" Ella slapped him over the back of the head for that.

Afterwards, however, we noticed how much cleaner and lighter the air became. Our spirits brightened too.

Dad, John and I cleared the furniture on the large back verandah to create an open space in the centre. There we dropped large cushions, five of them, and Gloria rehung a wind chime with tones similar to the singing bowl which I recognised once hung there before Mum and Anne-maree died. When I mentioned it to Gloria, an expression, familiar for some unknown reason I couldn't place, appeared on her face. I couldn't place it. Then she smiled and enigmatically said, "I know". The way she smiled, the twinkle in her eyes. I felt she was telling me something in the subtle way women can do without getting to the point because they like to challenge men to think. The wheels in my head hard just started to grind when Dad called us inside.

We woke at 5:30am each morning then meditated for ten-to-twenty minutes on the back verandah. Next we ran for five kilometres in the hot morning stillness. That was the only time he allowed us to leave our property, and we were to carry our stones with us always. Without exceptions. Upon returning, we would shower and eat breakfast. Then we would practise our shielding and mind-defence techniques.

The basic methods involved redirection of a mind attack's energy - similar to aikido or tai chi. For that, Dad showed us how to create what he called thought bolts. That took too long, so instead he focused on teaching us to sense and deflect (or reflect) them.

A question burned in my mind. Why do we have to practise this when we have protection stones?" I asked. "Stones have limits when carried on your person. I will teach you to use the one thing she can't take from you: your mind." We would practise our shielding and deflecting all day and stop only to eat, drink water. And when we ate, he said, we would eat vegetables, lots of them, with beans, lentils, and other plant-based proteins. No meat, no dairy, no alcohol (Gloria giggled at Dad on this one), and no processed junk. Ella and John gawked at me in bewilderment. I had never felt so embarrassed by my father!

The first morning was the worst. My normal practice was to rise at 6 am, even in winter. But 5:30am am seemed too early, and the pillow called me. I tried sneaking another few winks. My ploy soon ended when something caught my ear, and I opened my eyes in time to see water dropping from a glass above me. It splashed into my shocked mouth and across my face. I protested, but Ella just raised her eyebrows. "No way am I letting you sleep in if I can't," she said, and I heard the others laugh.

Lack of sleep wasn't our biggest issue. Our stomachs growled and begged for meat like the Mogwai from Gremlins grizzling for food after midnight.

As we continued, our bodies adapted to the diet, and we gradually discovered we could run easier without stopping as often - thanks to the strategy my father taught us. We became calmer, better focused. "You're still not as good as you need to be," Dad told me, "but you're all closer than if you hadn't done this. I hope it's enough." Then he pressed harder.

The only one allowed not to meditate all day was John. Neither Ella nor I learned what he did. He never told us; neither did Gloria nor Dad. But while Ella, Dad, Gloria, and I meditated out the back, John would venture inside to the living room. All doors to the room remained shut. Sometimes his voice floated through the cracks to the outside. The walls muffled his words to unintelligible syllables, but it sounded conversational, punctuated by occasional clicking sounds. When he showed for lunch, another meal of beans, lentils, fruit and vegetables, he said nothing of what he did, so the mystery deepened. How did he avoid meditation and shielding practice?

Dad kept me home on the weekend, too. He told my boss I was sick, which felt awkward to me. I'd never lie to my boss, thanks to the strong work ethic Dad infused in me, but he said it was necessary.

At last, the day before we visited Norman came.

# CHAPTER 33

Something wakened me from my dream of Norman. As my mind woke and realised it was a dream, I wondered at the night's deathlike stillness. Did I wake because I dreamed of Norman or was it the other thing that piqued my senses? I slowed my breathing, my ears alert for the slightest sound.

The silvery beams from the street light permeated the front windows, past the front sun room, and bounced into the living room. The couch upon which I rested escaped the light, shielded by the angles. I sensed the presence before it glided from my bedroom towards my couch.

"Ella?" I whispered upon recognising her. "What are you doing up?"

She knelt beside my improvised bed, placed her hand on my face and leaned to caress me in the darkness. I was alert in an instant. Blood flowed and pooled in my crotch as she gently lay on top of me, her lips seeking mine as we continued kissing. Embarrassed at my adolescent enthusiasm, I tried to move. Cramped down there, my member craved release. Noting the spontaneous growth, Ella's hand brushed over the area with curiosity, and there her hand lingered before a quiet giggle escaped her tender lips. Our gentle kisses matured and grew in earnestness, hungrier, but -

Ella's breathy whisper in my ear reflected my initial concern. "Your Dad and Gloria might come out. Follow me."

She clasped my hand, fingers interlocking, and we tiptoed back to the welcome familiarity and privacy of my bedroom and soon became more familiar with each other.

# CHAPTER 34

I awoke the following morning on the sofa with a foggy head. Vague memories of the night's events teased my mind like a dream, so I wondered if I dreamt them.

I rolled over and squinted in the early morning light at my digital watch's LCD screen.

4:45 am.

The others would wake soon, I figured, as I rose to my feet and trudged to the toilet. A part of me craved to visit Ella before the others woke. But Dad might discover me there and get the wrong (or right) idea, so I decided not.

The shower's frigid water shocked my skin, coerced a staccato tune from my chattering teeth. Soon wakefulness came to exorcise the floating images of my nocturnal activities from my mind. It didn't stop the smile stretching across my face until after I turned off the water and stepped dripping onto the floor-mat to towel myself dry.

Sounds from the waking household permeated the closed bathroom door. Gloria chatted to John about something. Ella's footsteps padded past the door and down the hallway, pausing for a moment before she entered the kitchen. Then came a knock on the door a moment before I twisted the handle to join them.

Dad's keen eyes gazed at me, a faint smirk tweaking the corners of his mouth. "How did you sleep last night?"

A sudden silence filled the kitchen as its occupants stopped to listen to my awkward reply. "With both eyes shut?"

Dad uttered a quiet snort and excused himself to enter the bathroom.

Gloria and John, both of whom caught Dad's words, continued eating their breakfast like nothing happened. Meanwhile, Ella's hands veiled her face.

*Oh, boy.*

As embarrassed as Ella, I sat beside her, too nervous and ashamed to glance at her, and ate my breakfast in silence. Gloria looked like she wanted to say something. But being an outsider, she clamped her mouth shut. John smirked under a raised eyebrow before engrossing himself in his breakfast of fruits.

"Hey," I said. "We haven't gone for our run before breakfast. I forgot..."

Dad entered the kitchen. "We're doing something different this morning. Let's visit Norman today."

John, Ella and I both looked up in surprise.

"Today?" Ella said.

Dad nodded. "Yes, but first..."

སྐལ་པ་

The crazy part is I remember little more of that morning. Just vague recollections of Norman's face, John's voice telling me something, a weightless sensation, and even some fatigue.

The next thing I recall is walking up the hospital wing's front steps and into the large foyer that reminded me of a Catholic church's interior without the pews. Near the front reception desk stood a Jesus Christ statue, his dead eyes staring at all who passed.

Everything else was normal as Ella, John, Dad, Gloria and I walked through the corridors until we reached Norman's wing. Almost everything.

The first thing we spotted was a trail of dark blood that marked a thread from further down the corridor towards Norman's room before it turned as if the person carrying it stopped to talk to someone before entering.

An involuntary shudder passed through me and my eyes, wide with concern, at the surreal atmosphere. Nursing staff walked the corridor as though not caring about the slippery crimson veins on the linoleum floor. One slipped in the blood, splattering the wall, and stood again after wiping her white dress which soon bore its stain before continuing as though nothing strange had happened.

"Is this real?" Ella's words quivered and choked.

Paled-faced, John gulped hard and nodded. "I'm not eating meat again."

"Can't the staff see what's happening around them?" I said, grasping the stone cradled in my pocket.

But the scene remained as bloody and sickening as before.

"She's clouded the hospital's minds to everything," Gloria said.

One of the staff at the ward's nursing station looked up and smiled. A smear of blood glistened from her lips as she spoke. "May I help you?"

"No, thank you," my father replied with a voice. I admired his ability to remain placid despite the surrounding atrocities. "Come along, kids."

He led us to Norman's door. The pool of putrid blood reflected my shocked face. I tried avoiding the mess, but that proved impossible.

Dad faced us all with a serious glare. His eyes radiated a powerful sense of focus that calmed us. "Gloria and John, stay here. Ella, Robin, we're going in."

I stole a moment to glance at Ella. She returned my gaze with an equally fearful expression. In that moment, the strongest desire express my thoughts and feelings for her overwhelmed me.

"I love you," I whispered to her.

"I love you too."

"Come on," Dad prodded us. "We're running out of time."

We took and held a deep breath for a few seconds before exhaling before entering the room for the last time.

# CHAPTER 35

In stark contrast to the scene outside, Norman's room appeared cleaner. Yet what created the bloody trail in the hall soon became clear the moment we entered. On the windowsill sat a head with a shock of red hair, its face looking out the window towards the front street. We teenagers gasped upon recognising Richard Crane's features.

Beside him, her face pale and white like the moon with purple trailing veins, sat Norman's mother. Her lips opened in a grin laced with green teeth upon seeing us.

"Robin!" Her voice sounded raw, husky, like Stevie Nicks only sinister. "How delightful of you to grace us with your presence." She nodded towards Richard. "We just said how one can always tell true friends when we're in tough times." Mrs Cole motioned towards the other corner. "Matthew visited today too to offer his apologies."

I glanced towards the other wall. Where a clock once sat, hung what looked like a mask. The more I scrutinised it, the more I realised the worst. The scrappy shock of white-blond hair struck me as familiar. Something, or someone, had ripped Matthew's face and scalp off his head and hung it on the wall like a painting. Because it hung from a hook, nothing else supported the face which distorted much like the corpse of a busted balloon. The eyes, having no lids, gaped open to reveal the wall behind it.

"So nice of him to hang out with Norman, isn't it?"

Vomit bubbled up the back of my throat. I swallowed it back in time to avoid throwing up, but the acid hurt like stale lemonade. "Nice to see you too, Mrs Cole," I replied.

"Where is that nice (she lisped that word) boy John?" she answered. "He has yet to visit Norman too."

"He's -"

Dad nudged Ella. "Ruth, you need to wake. Fight

Maerie's influence."

Mrs Cole glared hard at Dad. "What do you care? Maerie's been honest with me, and she's shown what a loyal girl she is to my Norman." She regarded Ella with a cold stare. "Unlike his sister who hasn't visited in a week."

"Mum, I-"

"And your father won't visit either."

While Ella and Dad distracted Mrs Cole, I sneaked my way to Norman's side. Matthew's shredded, eyeless face glared at me as I placed my headphones over Norman's ears. For a moment, a memory flashed across my mind of the last time I saw him at the water-slide. The plump face he once had no longer existed. Despite how I disliked his character, I missed Matthew. The same for Richard Crane whose head and spinal column hung on the windowsill like a mutant tadpole.

My distraction was all Mrs Cole needed. With a bloodcurdling cry, she lunged for me; her sharp fingernails on long fingers that aimed for my windpipe. Without thinking, I flooded white light from myself in a psychic shield. I surprised myself with my reflex. But it didn't stop her. I panicked, more-so when Ella screamed, backpedalled to avoid her, and tripped backward against the wall. Mrs Cole moved fast. Thankfully, Dad moved faster.

In a single fluid motion, he blocked Mrs Cole's advance and locked one of her arms. Despite her attempt to dislodge him, Dad gripped the side of her neck and squeezed.

Mrs Cole's eyes flickered a moment and closed, her screams quietened, and she dropped unconscious in his arms.

"I didn't know you could do a Vulcan Grip," I said, breathing hard.

"It's just a nerve pinch." Dad gently lowered the sleeping Mrs Cole to the ground. "The things you have yet to learn about me could fill an encyclo-" He groaned and crumpled to the ground.

Before I realised it, Maerie appeared from nowhere and stood over my father's prone figure. She wound her foot to kick him in the side, but Dad's own foot lashed into Maerie's ankle. She stumbled back straight into Ella who smashed a convenient vase on her head.

Instead of falling, Maerie stood for a moment, blinking, and turned to face Ella who delivered another punch to the tulpa's face. Then it was on stronger than Vegemite on toast. Both Ella and Dad lashed with psychic and physical attacks at Maerie.

For my part, I felt obsessed with Norman and reached into my backpack for the Walkman and headphones from before. My heart raced, pumping adrenaline through me, which made my fingers fumble. Despite this, my mind felt clear. I didn't know why but the uncontrollable urge to place the headphone on Norman's ears. A glass of water flew past my head to smash into wet smithereens against the wall behind me. I ducked to avoid another missile and pressed Play.

The Walkman purred to life, its green power light eliciting a smile before I glanced at the fight in time to witness Ella's body slam into the wall. She moaned, her eyes rolled back in her head, and slumped to the floor.

In a flash, Maerie darted to Ella's dazed body and held her finger to my girlfriend's throat. The nails became talons and pressed against the delicate skin. Maerie gave us a warning glare.

"Did you think your silly black stones would stop me?" Maerie's voice roared like a death metal singer's death growl.

Dad and I paused for a moment.

"Let her go."

Maerie directed her withering gaze upon Dad and repeated her growl. "Get out!" She pressed Ella's throat, producing the slightest trickle of red, which she caught on her claw and brought to her waiting tongue. "One dumb-arse move, and she dies."

Dad's gaze never left the tulpa. He clenched and released his jaw, his temples pulsing like a brain-beat.

"Robin, leave the room."

I took a step.

Maerie shouted. "No! You stay here, Robin." Spittle splattered from her mouth in force.

Bewildered, I froze as Maerie regarded Dad. "You leave, Mr Mitchell... Father."

Dad's calm voice contrasted with the creature's fury. "You may appear like my daughter. But that's all."

"Go! Or... she... dies."

They both eyed each other, father and wannabe-daughter. For a moment, I suspected Maerie to be my sister returned from the void. She even possessed the same defiant bitch-from-hell expression as when Anne-maree beheaded my Steve Austin doll. Her nostrils flared and the nose-ring danced like a mad cartoon bull. Dad stared back, outwardly placid as a pond.

At last, Dad breathed deep and relaxed with slightly slumping shoulders. He looked away from her to regard me. For a moment, he seemed to calculate something and glanced at Norman then back at me. Sad uncertainty radiated from his eyes. "I'm sorry, Robin."

"What?"

Disgusted betrayal hit me hard until I caught his wink. Then calm hope filled me.

"I must go."

He slowly walked past Maerie and out the door. In my mind, calmness remained. Yet my heart hammered like hell's bones accompanied by Maerie's chuckle of triumphant delight.

# CHAPTER 36

A sardonic smile crossed Maerie's face, and her eyes glinted, as Dad quit the room. With a flick of her fingers, the door shut, then she faced me and laughed as she stood.

"Alone at last."

Perhaps I should have been fearful at that point. The tulpa possessed enough will power to flatten me like a pancake under a steamroller. But reasons I didn't understand, my head remained clear and functional. I shrugged.

"Except for your in-laws and Norman."

Maerie's eyes flashed as she approached me. I side-stepped, expecting I don't know what, but she passed towards Matthew Stubbs' death mask. Her fingers brushed along the atrocity as she pondered something. "This Matthew was the most fun to kill," she said. "I know you detested him."

"Not enough to kill."

"Doesn't matter," she snapped back. "Such a manipulative shit. Do you know he kept files on everyone?" Her watchful gaze bore into me, eliciting little more than a shrug from me. "Yes, he did. He learned people's weaknesses, directed them to do his dirty work, and to shut them up he blackmailed them." She ripped the skin and flesh from the hook and waved it aloft as she spoke. "I loved ripping off his face as much as cutting off his genitals and choking him with the pieces. Matt, Matt, Matt." Her eyes measured my lack of response, and a grin appeared as she dropped Matthew's face so it landed like a sheet. She chuckled and stepped on the skin to wipe her feet. "Mat," she giggled.

I ignored her sick joke. As her features darkened, I realised my lack of response unhinged her. A potential weakness? I turned my attention towards Mrs Cole.

In sleep, Mrs Cole appeared the picture of her usual self. Smooth skin that shone from too much Oil of Ulan, which stressed her skin's wrinkles (rather than hide them). Hair unkempt from who knows how much time spent in the hospital without visiting home. Her clothes looked like she'd been sleeping in the hospital room the whole time. Purple veins no longer maligned her countenance.

I lifted her from the floor to sit her in the chair beside Norman's bed. No way would I let her remain on the ground.

"You're too kind to her," Maerie said, stepping around in a rough circle as she watched me approach Ella. "She hates the prospect of her children liking you more than her."

"Sounds like the perfect mother-in-law," I replied and checked Ella's vitals. Her carotid pulse beat regularly under my fingers, so I lifted her gently to place in the other chair. "She seems to like you though." Maerie gave a pleased smile at that. "Too bad she has no taste, like you said."

Instinct lifted my hand and amazed me upon finding I had caught a dagger millimetres from my eye. Its long steel blade point glinted in the sunlight from outside. Another spark shone followed by another, and another. Quicker than my conscious thoughts processed, my hand deflected each new dagger Maerie conjured from the air towards me.

Ting, ting, tang.

The steel bladed missiles, each with three triangular faces, clattered to the hard floor at my feet.

I looked across at Maerie and allowed myself a smile at her surprised expression before examining the knife in my hand. Heavy in my hand, I awed at the blade's length and triangular design as long as the handle, decorated with a strange face on the end. The handle bent like a neck, allowing the long-faced vicious face to poke its tongue at me as it glared into my eyes.

With a sudden twist, the knife whipped from my hand and into the air to spin like a crazy compass needle. Or maybe like the spinning bottle in the game, only it promised a kiss of death upon pointing at me.

A blur of motion, the dagger zoomed towards me again. This time, I didn't catch it. The blade stopped short of my raised hand, blocked by my thoughts.

Maerie's face reflected my disbelief and amazement. My six days of training never covered combat by Tibetan dagger. But the tulpa's surprised cry emboldened me, and with a flick of my finger, I launched the weapon back at her face.

"You don't belong here, Maerie."

Maerie screamed and ducked the blade which stuck fast in the wall. Her shocked eyes stared at me a second, calculating, before she waved her hand. "So let's leave."

The room disappeared, bloodstained walls and floors replaced by a blackness dotted with bright sparks that provided colour and minimal light. There I floated in ... nothingness. A weightless sensation overcame me. I couldn't tell up from down.

"You have killed everyone who bullied Norman," I shouted into the darkness. "What more do you want?"

Her voice, venom to the heart, whispered in my ear. "Your death."

A tingling sensation touched the back of my mind. I fortified my psychic shield, pressed back at whatever prodded me, repelled it. She cursed, but this time her voice came from metres away in the opposite direction.

"My death? Why?"

"Because you wished me dead." The voice passed me the way stereo headphones sometimes do.

"You?" I laughed. "You are not real. Only a thought-form."

"Not now. Years ago."

My eyebrow arched. Now I knew what Maerie found in my head when she last invaded my mind.

"You're describing a childhood memory. The thoughts of an immature little boy."

"Yet you killed me. And so I shall kill... You." This time the voice spoke in my left ear. Her breath passed across my throat a moment before a hot stabbing pain lanced through my side.

The pained gasp escaped me in a rush. As soon as my hands reached my aching side, my mind re-fortified its shield. Amazed at my self-control, I glanced at my hand. Nothing. No blood. Another illusion.

"Yet I live." The words came in a simple sentence stripped of emotion. A plain fact. "Your illusions can't hurt me."

An instant later, the blackness disappeared, and I was back in the hospital room again. An ethereal breeze blasted me and the room; Maerie's hair flowed in it like a mad river. I shielded my eyes to see better against the heat.

There it was.

The Tibetan dagger.

Its blade's triangular faces resembling a misshapen Philips head screwdriver.

Spinning like a battered weather-vane.

I took a relaxing breath, squinted against the breeze, and prepared for the dagger's swift deadly strike.

But, no!

It had another target. Too late, I sprang to stop it.

Its deadly momentum proved too fast.

Too late, I cried in vain.

Ella!

The hungry dagger's blade pierced her unconscious chest and ploughed straight through her left breast.

I screamed tears. Emotion, cold and hard, raged through my core. My shield disappeared. I didn't care.

In a moment, I sat by her side and pressed my fingers hard to stem the hot blood pumping from her chest. Crimson life squirted between my fingers to spill over me.

"No!"

And the she-demon Maerie, for lack of a better term, stood in the corner and laughed. "No," she mimicked me, falsetto-voiced. "Not my girlfriend."

I held onto Ella, wishing her eyes would open,

praying was another illusion. But inside I knew. It was real.

I dared not remove the dagger. A quiet voice in my head said what will be, will be. To remove the dagger will speed her demise by unblocking the vein and kill her quicker.

In that horrific moment, another voice entered my head.

Ella's voice.

But it wasn't Ella.

The voice came from the corner.

I shifted my gaze to towards a new Ella. Her beautiful hair showering over bare shoulders. Naked skin reflecting the golden sunlight from the window. Bare breasts with erect nipples. And her hands on her hips, one of them sliding towards the place between her legs.

"Do you want me, Robin?" Her voice, cruel and mocking, proved seductive enough to shift my loins with desire.

But Ella's weight in my arms returned to my mind. I regarded her closed eyelids, her skin already turning white.

The she-demon persisted from the corner. "I can be yours, Robin. Norman will die anyway."

I'm not sure what ticked me off the most. Norman's self-professed girlfriend trying to seduce me while standing beside him as he lay comatose? Or perhaps my guilty temptation upon seeing the fantasy of my love before me for which I hated myself. Or her mocking me, Ella and Norman at once.

"Come, come for me, Robbie," she crooned. "Experience passion like no other with me while our partners are gone."

Mount Tambo and Krakatoa couldn't compare to my anger which reduced Chernobyl to a fart in a bathtub.

"Passion?" I spat. "PASSION?"

A triumphant smile crossed Maerie's face. She said nothing, just smiled, mockingly, as the blood pumped to my face.

"I'll show you passion, you bloody bitch!"

I bent my face towards Ella's cold lips and warmed them with my own. Careful not to hurt her, I lathered her with the love I held for her. The coolness of Ella's dying lips didn't deter me, and for a moment, she didn't respond. Yet for a sweet moment, her eyes opened, her lips moved a little in response to me, ever so weakly.

Surprise filled me, but the bonus came next.

For the tulpa's influence weakened. Through the angry tears that stung my eyes, I gazed at the creature's mouth gaped in surprise. Silent words moved her lips and a soft whimper escaped her throat. "What?"

So came my opportunity.

When the creature stepped backward in mute shock, I gently rested my girlfriend's head against the wall, telling her to rest. I kissed her again, loving the notion of Ella's recovery, and stood to face Maerie.

Never had I hit a woman until that day. While Maerie floundered at my recovery, I stepped in and belted the bitch across the face. Her blood spattered across the wall and onto Norman's pillow. A scarlet drop hit his nose. My other hand delivered an uppercut to her chin which caused her teeth to chatter and chip.

But there was fight left in the monster as she punched me hard with an unseen bolt of energy. For a moment, I flew. Fast.

Pain flared in my shoulders as I hit the wall and landed next to Ella. Another explosion echoed my back radiating towards my shoulders and legs. I screamed, tears flooded my vision, and I realised my hands wouldn't move.

Blood continued to run from Maerie's busted nose and mouth as she stood there, panting hard. One hand lifted, wiped it, and flicked the mess at me as she approached. Unable to stop her, my frozen limbs refused to budge as Maerie lifted Ella by the collar and punched her hard in the stomach. Another bone-cracking blow landed on Ella's face, hard enough to create horrible sounds. Ella's head smacked backward with the punch like a balloon before slumping forward.

Maerie's eyes studied Ella's inert form, smiled at the blood that poured from Ella's face and splattered on her shoes, before dropping her to the ground. "She's not so pretty now."

Tears in my eyes gushed upon seeing Ella's lifeless yet open eyes gaze at me from my lap. I tried to hold her close, but I couldn't move. Something was wrong. Something bad. I wept.

"Oh," Maerie's mocking voice rang. "Is little Robbie's back broken so he can't cuddle his wench's dead body?"

Defeated, I said nothing. Just cried. I wished I had never heard of tulpas and wept more. For a moment, I even considered Dad's warning to avoid Norman, that nothing good would come of it.

Maerie lifted me by my shoulders and glared hard into my eyes while my feet dangled like limp noodles. I couldn't hold my head up. It was Maerie's power that kept me staring back at her. Blinded by the pain in my spine, I barely saw through my half-closed eyelids and the tears. Part of me wanted to beat the shit out of Maerie's face and throat for killing Ella. But my limbs refused to ball a fist, let alone smack her down. I couldn't even kick.

"My poor brother." Maerie's condescending voice rang. "As useless as his childhood Steve Austin doll." Then her lips touched mine. The flicking tongue produced the desire to yak in her mouth.

"Yet I am merciful, big brother. I can't let you suffer. Do you have any last words?"

Then came the miracle.

# CHAPTER 37

"Maerie."

The unexpected voice paused the tulpa, her shocked eyes the size of Monte Carlo biscuits. Fear flicked in her voice, mixed with relief, and flood her face.

The Creator had spoken.

Although weak, his voice possessed an angry strength. So familiar, long unheard, and cutting, his voice made me wet my pants with relief. Or maybe my broken spinal column did. "Put Robin down. Carefully."

Maerie froze, a hesitancy in her action.

"Please do it now, Maerie."

"Norman?" I whispered, not daring to accept..

Still gripping my arms with steel hands, Maerie turned towards the voice. There Norman sat, propped upright against the pillows and wide awake. One thin white hand reached to pull the headphones from his ears.

"Thanks for the tunes, Robin," he said. His eyes, blurry without his glasses, focused on Maerie. "I told you to put my friend down."

Maerie hesitated further, speechless.

"Now."

Maerie turned toward an overturned chair and blinked to make it stand and lowered me into it. Pain lanced through me again which prompted another cry from my tortured throat. A baleful light flickered from her angry eyes as she regarded me before she returned her attention to her boyfriend and creator.

Her voice, soft and loving. "Norman! You're awake!"

She hurried to Norman to cover his face in kisses. His fingers flinched as though to return the favour, but he didn't.

"You tried to seduce Robin, my best friend," he said, glancing at me a moment before eyeballing her with naked anger.

Maerie faltered. "But nothing happened."

"You killed my sister and tortured my mother too." Although weak, Norman's hands possessed enough strength to push Maerie away from him.

The tulpa faltered. "I -"

"And you killed Jason, Lou, Paul, and the others."

"For you, my love."

Norman's eyes hardened, his jaw tensed a moment, then he exploded. "You did killed for yourself, your jealousy, and your --- your ---"

"I did it for you, to be together forever with you when you woke. Can't you see?" Maerie's panicked voice rose high and hurt my ears.

Norman's face remained still, never flinching, as she delivered her honey-coated lies.

When he spoke, his voice so cold, I blinked to be sure it really was my friend.

"You're dropped."

Maerie gasped. Her lips formed a perfect O, a silent scream, as she dissolved before my eyes. Her skin darkened, turned pitch black to match her hair and dress. The nose-ring dropped from her withering face and landed on the floor before rolling towards my feet which I still couldn't feel. A breeze gusted from nowhere and blew Maerie's fine dusty remains to nothingness.

Soon everything turned still. I tried to shift, but my limbs refused to budge.

Norman stared into space for a few seconds, his face hard, a tear rolling down his face. Unsure what happened, I waited, unable to move. Then he faced me, pushed back the sheet from himself, and grunted. With some effort, he pivoted and exited the bed on wobbly legs. One hand gripped the bed as he steadied himself.

One painful step at a time, he approached me and knelt beside Ella. With gentle fingers, he stroked the loose hair from her face, his face glistening with tears. Then he choked back a sob. "I'm sorry, Ella. I hoped you'd be strong enough to see."

"She did," I replied through my own tears and wracked crying. "She realised what Maerie was before I did."

Norman lifted his face, crawled towards my chair, and lifted himself to stand near me. He lifted my hand in his own. I cried harder.

"I can't feel your hand."

Shocked, he nodded. "I'm sorry, Robbo. It's all my fault. Can you forgive me?"

I said nothing. Ella's deathly stillness filled my vision and thoughts, and I grieved for lost love.

"She loved you too," Norman said. "She whispered to me once how she loved you while I slept. Everything's hard to tell, but she told me. You kept the secret from me all those years, but I know you loved her too."

"Why?" I asked, emotion battling logic. "Why did you do it?"

Norman shrugged. His eyes shifted, lowered. "I was lonely."

"No. Why did you make her kill the others? Because they put you in the coma?"

"What?" Norman cocked his head in surprise and paused. "No. I didn't make her kill. Nor did they put me in the coma. Maerie did it all."

"Say what?" My tears disappeared a moment in surprise.

"Yes, I bumped into Lou Patch, Paul, and Jason too. But friendlier than before. They were more interested in their new lives after high school. They even waved at me from their car as they drove past me on Boundary Road. Scared me at first, but what a relief when I realised."

I said nothing. Unable to nod, I blinked. Norman continued. "When I reached the top of the hill near the bridge. She... Maerie... She appeared in front of me, and she looked mad and angry. Angry at me. Next thing I find myself flying into the bushes and down the river bank. Next everything goes black. And I'm in darkness for ages.

Sometimes sounds come to me, like your voice, Mum or Ella's. Then Maerie whispers in my ears and head, telling me all --"

Screams from the hallway outside cut off Norman's story. He turned towards the sounds, puzzlement on his face.

"Maerie left a mess outside in the hall," I explained, upon remembering the earlier events. "The bloody trail in here came from outside. It's everywhere.

"And they're just screaming now?"

The disbelief in his voice made me laugh. I don't know why. "Maerie hypnotised everyone."

Norman's brow furrowed a moment before he nodded his understanding.

Soon after, the door opened. Dad and Gloria came in, accompanied by a security guard. They stopped in horror at the scene before them. Gloria burst into tears upon seeing my broken and battered body and ran towards me.

"Mrs Mitchell?" Norman said in surprise. "How -?"

"That's Gloria," I explained. "Dad's new girlfriend."

"Gloria?" Norman shook his head. "No, mate, she's your Mum. See the birthmark on her throat?"

"What?" My eyes searched, but Gloria sat too close for me to check.

"It doesn't matter," Dad said as Gloria held me tight, and surprise crossed my mind.

# CHAPTER 38

Questions. Heaps of questions filled my mind.

I learned that Gloria is my mother. Dad had tried to tell me, but John and Ella's arrival interrupted him. The opportunity lost, he decided it could wait. Years back, after the accident killed Anne-maree, Mum sat in hospital with her own injuries and grief. She wouldn't talk to Dad. In fact, she spoke to no one and remained silent, catatonic. The accident wasn't her fault - a drunk driver had rammed her car - but she took the responsibility in her mind. I didn't fully understand why, but thirty years later, I understand grief does strange things to people.

Dad never told me the full story then thinking me too young to understand yet. When Mum disappeared without telling him, he ended up telling me she had died. He explained it was easier... until Mum returned under an assumed name and found a job at town hall. It took her close to ten years to work up the courage to talking to Dad again, but she wanted her life in order first in case he rejected her.

Luckily, Dad was as faithful as a penguin and still mourned Mum and Anne-maree.

The authorities couldn't make head or tail of the mess in the hospital. No one did. The Daily Sentinel published the stories for the next week or two until after Christmas and New Year. Upon seeing me injured in the hospital room with an injured back, the police discounted me as a suspect. No way could I kill so many unnoticed. The focus fell upon Norman, but comatose people don't do nothing but sleep, right? We defended each other as mates do, then we defended Norman's mother when they blamed her.

The poor woman. Still catatonic years later, Mrs Cole does nothing but sit in a chair and stares at the corner.

Sometimes she rocks back and forth with drool dropping from her mouth. I hate to speculate what will happen when - or if - she recovers. Mr Cole visited her daily until he died of a heart attack in 2015. Now she sits alone, oblivious to the others in the old people's home, not even noticing when Norman visits and holds her hand.

Eventually, lacking solid leads, the police placed the incident in the cold case archive. But I can't help wondering what they found on a camera's video footage. Did they even see Maerie as she splashed her bloody victims about in the hospital wing?

And Norman. Well, what a sleeper he turned out to be.

Then there's John. What a dude. With his father being a psychologist and hypnotherapist, it didn't take John much to develop an interest in hypnosis. Dad cottoned onto that pretty quickly and that's how he developed his backup plan in case we failed to beat Maerie. While Ella and I were training on psychic shields, he had John create a special mix-tape. But not just any tape. John had created a subliminal tape with hidden messages in its recording. So while anyone listening to it would think it was just heaps of songs, Norman's subconscious mind was also listening to the hidden messages telling him to wake up, to "absorb" Maerie back, to uncreate her.

That's not all.

There's a whole day of my memory wiped clean from the day before we visited Norman and confronted Maerie. That's the day when Dad had Ella, John, and me listen to another tape John created. A hypnosis tape. Besides specially encoding our fighting plan, John designed the messages to hide any other information from Maerie if she invaded our minds again.

Dad felt he didn't need the hypnosis, but he also left the room to let us do our job. He just couldn't save Ella. He still regrets it to this day.

Ella.

My beautiful girlfriend. She had a beautiful funeral service at the North Middleville Crematorium on Old Farm Road. Her many friends and family attended. Mr Cole looked so broken. I felt sorry for him and remembered the morning we spoke to him outside his workplace. A part of me regretted failing him. Poor beautiful and brilliant Ella. If only I could grow old with her.

Unable to walk, Norman and I were wheelchair buddies. His muscles had atrophied, and my spinal column remained swollen. I couldn't speak for Ella at the service. All I could do was look at her wooden coffin on the conveyor belt while the minister gave his sermon in the little chapel.

I'd give anything for Ella to have survived.

# CHAPTER 39

Unable to operate on my back, the doctors said I'd be wheelchair-bound for life. Assisted walking only once the swelling receded. No more bike riding, cricket, or even basketball. The pain was unbearable. Each step torturous. Although elated when my hands worked again, I tired fast and had to rest a lot. Concentrating on school proved difficult.

People's attitudes towards me changed too. At shopping centres, they "didn't see me". They'd cut in front of my wheelchair when I tried to check something in the shops. Even assistants would talk to Dad or Mum… Gloria… before they talked to me. If they did, they spoke in condescending tones or pitiful expressions. Like the wheelchair or something had damaged my brain.

Dad and Gloria/Mum talked. Sometimes they fought at night. About me. At night, I'd listen through the bedroom wall to their bickering and frustration.

At last, they worked things out between them. They uprooted me from everything I knew - my home, my friends, and school - to take me to a certain Tibetan monastery. The one where they had first met.

There I learned to meditate. It proved difficult at first. But thirty-four years later, I meditate well. The monks taught me techniques to surpass my pain, to embrace and befriend it, to live, and to control it rather than the opposite. On my twentieth birthday, I took my first pain-free steps. Another six months later, I walked ten miles. Now, I walk whenever and wherever I wish.

I only return to Middleville for Christmas with Norman who has since become a computer security guru and John, and my aunty Deb. Because they're such close friends, people assumed Norman and John an item, but they're not.

སྦྲལ་བ་

I sense her presence, quiet and careful, before her soft footsteps tease the grass. Without turning towards her, I know she stands behind me, straight and refined in a black tailored pantsuit as she waits for me to finish my meditation.

A stray notion intrudes. I push it away, but not before I recognise the image, and open my eyes.

"Hello, Ella," I say, still not turning to face her.

She gasps in surprise. "You recognise me?"

I allow a smile, one of my brightest since I left Middleville, and turn toward her. Yes, she wears the same clothing I saw in my mind.

She looks lovely. Gone are the youthful teenage years, replaced by the growing sophistication of a young journalist in her late twenties. Dawn's golden rays dance from her smooth skin and reflect in her eyes. Such a contrast to my orange robes since I joined the monastery. So different to our adolescent days.

Ella smiles. Her eyes sparkle and reflect the sun. Yet she hesitates. I return her smile and open my arms with a nod. She moves forward and squeezes me the way I remember. At first, I lose myself in the blissful embrace, teenage thoughts and memories of my first kiss with her flood my mind. Old memories stir my loins. But I push them back, conscious of the consequences, and escape the hug.

For this Ella casts no shadow.

# A FINAL NOTE

There is more to the mysteries of tulpamancy than I wrote in Norman and Robin's tale.

If you wish to learn more, visit <u>https://chrisjohnsonauthor.blogspot.com/1988/01/tulpas.html</u>

# ABOUT THE AUTHOR

Born in the city of Rockhampton, Central Queensland, Chris Johnson grew up on a diet of Atari computers, comics, and nineteen-eighties television. Today he lives in Brisbane with his own family.
When not writing, Chris performs as a mentalist and psychic entertainer at corporate and private functions. He also enjoys watching movies, reading, running, and kung fu.

**You can find Chris at:**
**Facebook:**
https://www.facebook.com/ChrisJohnsonAuthor
and
**his website**
https://chrisjohnsonauthor.blogspot.com.au

# OTHER BOOKS BY CHRIS JOHNSON

Twelve Strokes of Midnight

CRAIG RAMSEY SERIES
Dead Cell
Demon Blade

Bootstrap's Journey
While He Was Sleeping

# WHILE HE WAS SLEEPING